THE SECRET EMPRESS

FRANK R. HELLER

iUniverse®

THE SECRET EMPRESS

iUniverse books may be ordered through booksellers or by contacting:

iUniverse
1663 Liberty Drive
Bloomington, IN 47403
www.iuniverse.com
1-800-Authors (1-800-288-4677)

Because of the dynamic nature of the Internet, any web addresses or links contained in
this book may have changed since publication and may no longer be valid. The views
expressed in this work are solely those of the author and do not necessarily reflect the
views of the publisher, and the publisher hereby disclaims any responsibility for them.

This is a work of fiction. All of the characters, names, incidents, organizations, and dialogue
in this novel are either the products of the author's imagination or are used fictitiously.

Any people depicted in stock imagery provided by Getty Images are models,
and such images are being used for illustrative purposes only.
Certain stock imagery © Getty Images.

ISBN: 978-1-5320-6832-4 (sc)
ISBN: 978-1-5320-6831-7 (hc)
ISBN: 978-1-5320-6830-0 (e)

Library of Congress Control Number: 2019902407

Print information available on the last page.

iUniverse rev. date: 08/09/2019

For my incredible wife, Susan, our dear friend, Lea, and our grandchildren Zoe, Sophia, Josie and Jemma. Without Jemma's enthusiasm for this story, I probably would never have finished the manuscript.

Thank you

PROLOGUE

SAMMY LIN TWISTED THE THROTTLE OF THE MOTOR SCOOTER AS far as he could, trying to get as much speed as possible out of the 150 cc engine. Accelerating down the exit ramp of the parking structure, the little scooter hit the sidewalk and became airborne for thirty feet before it careened across three lanes of traffic. Even at three o'clock in the morning, Beijing traffic was not to be taken lightly. Fighting to keep control, Sammy swerved around a large truck, leaned too far to the left, and sideswiped the front fender of a Toyota as the driver slammed on the brakes. The scooter fishtailed violently—as did Sammy's heart rate. When he finally regained control, he turned south toward the Drum Tower.

For the first time since bolting from the meeting in the Bai Lang's penthouse, Sammy looked back to see whether they were following him. There were no big black sedans in sight, but that didn't matter. Sooner or later, they would send the German.

"The Bai Lang is crazy!" Sammy shouted into the wind. "That pig kept yelling that the last emperor had a child—find the child, find the child!"

Sammy suddenly hit the brakes and twisted the handlebar, sending the scooter skidding along the pavement, narrowly missing a minivan that cut him off.

"Everyone knows the last emperor had no children. Didn't he see the movie?"

As he neared the ancient Drum Tower, the flow of vehicles coming into the city thinned considerably. It would be a few more hours before the traffic would be a problem. For now, he had to get away from Beijing and away from the Bai Lang as fast as possible. He had some money hidden at his grandparents' house in the old Hutong section of the city. That was his escape—the money would get him away, out of the reach of the Bai Lang.

Twenty minutes later, Sammy cut the engine and parked the scooter around the corner from his grandparents' home. Only a few of the houses along the old narrow street were occupied, and even those were dark at this hour. There were no streetlights either, the only illumination coming from the full moon hanging low in the sky. He stood still for a few minutes, straining to hear anything out of the ordinary, but there was only silence and the pounding of his own heart.

Sammy walked along the street, staying as close to the buildings as possible. His destination was the third door down on the right. It was never locked; the key had been lost generations ago. Cautiously, he turned the knob, slowly pushed the door open, and took three steps into the room. Almost immediately, the door was slammed shut behind him.

"Come in, Sammy." The German switched on a table lamp, filling the room with a soft light. "We have been waiting for you. You have been telling our secrets to someone, Sammy, and the Bai Lang wants to know who."

ONE

MICHAEL FITZPATRICK STOOD IN THE CENTER OF HIS OFFICE, staring at the sea of city lights spread out beneath him. The office was on the eighth floor of the US embassy chancellery building and consisted of floor-to-ceiling windows that made up two of the four walls of his plush cubicle. From this vantage point, facing southwest, he had a 180-degree unobstructed view of the Beijing night skyline. He loved the way the Forbidden City and Tiananmen Square, not more than four or five miles away, seemed to shimmer in the wash of a hundred floodlights. Just off to the right, he could see the twin Drum and Water Towers lit up like beacons in the midst of the ancient neighborhoods. Behind the embassy complex, beyond the Third Ring Road, lay the newest of the high-rise buildings and Olympic stadiums that represented the modern growth of the city. But it was the vision of the old city at night, the panorama of lights and the muted city sounds, that Michael always found to be wonderfully soothing. Especially after spending two hours combing through the latest intelligence reports.

It's fascinating, he thought with a little laugh. *Even after three thousand years, this city has more spies, conspiracies, and intrigues than any other capital in the world.*

Roused from his reverie by the sound of his iPhone beeping, Michael realized that it was two in the morning, time to head down to the ops center.

Of the more than one thousand employees at the site, very few were aware that there was a strategic operations center within the US embassy in Beijing. It was a cavernous room hidden deep within the subterranean maze below the ten-acre footprint of the embassy complex. As he rode the elevator down to the security level, Michael Fitzpatrick calculated that over the last five years he'd spent more than half his time in the ops center as opposed to his office. Officially, he was listed on the embassy staff directory as the senior trade delegate. Unofficially, the secret personnel files at Langley listed Michael J. Fitzpatrick as the CIA station chief. In fact, he was, at forty-two, one of the youngest station chiefs in the service.

The Marine guard on duty scrutinized his ID, comparing the man standing before him with the image and statistics described on the badge and displayed on his computer screen. Over six feet tall, curly blond hair, lean and athletic, Fitzpatrick had the fashionable good looks that would have been at home on a photo shoot or movie set. His easy smile and amiable manner were valuable assets to someone in his profession.

"Are you new here, Corporal?"

"Yes, sir, transferred in Monday." Apparently satisfied, he pressed the electronic door release and handed back the ID badge.

"Did they give you the standard orientation speech?" Fitzpatrick asked.

"No, sir." The corporal smiled. "The watch commander just said to watch out for the hard-ass on the eighth floor."

"Just a little bit of a hard-ass." He returned the smile. "Please tell Master Gunnery Sergeant Maxwell that I'll give him a chance to get even at the poker game Thursday night."

"I'll relay the message, sir."

The ops center bore a striking resemblance to the trading floor of the New York Stock Exchange. However, the center was smaller and more intense and sometimes dealt in life and death. Three curved rows of desks, each with its own set of multiple-screen computer terminals, stood on raised platforms like stadium seats in a theater. A total of twenty-four desks faced a large electronic display screen that covered most of the eastern wall of the room. While the large screen showed a map of the world, six smaller screens—three at each end—presented live feeds from satellites in orbit around the globe. A series of small lights, some blinking rapidly while others glowed continuously, were scattered across the map. Their selection of color indicated the seriousness of conditions on the ground at any particular site.

Michael stopped to study the map for a moment.

"You got another late-night conference call, Mike?" Tony Pearson, the senior political analyst on duty, shook Michael's hand with a firm grip. He was short and about twenty pounds overweight, and he chewed gum incessantly to fight his craving for cigarettes. At fifty-six, he was nearing the end of his career with the State Department. "That makes three this week, doesn't it?"

"You know, just the routine stuff." He shrugged off the question. "What's going on in your world?"

"Well, it's all quiet on the western front and on the eastern front, but in the middle, we had two car bombs in Baghdad last night." The embassy rumor mill said that Tony considered himself to be far more amusing than anyone else in the room.

"So it's business as usual?"

"You could say that." The analyst turned his attention back to his computer screens. "Anyway, have fun."

Michael stopped at the service table to help himself to a cup of black coffee as he crossed the huge room to the secure communications unit.

"Your call is scheduled for 3:00 a.m. in the conference room, Mr. Fitzpatrick." The duty officer, Susan Harper, was a pretty young woman in her twenties. She, too, was newly assigned to the embassy. "Would you sign the log, please?"

"Thanks, Susan." Michael pushed the door closed securely after entering the room. Of the twelve chairs, he picked one at the middle of the table nearest the telephone console and stretched his long legs out onto the next chair. He checked his watch and then sipped the black coffee and waited.

"Your call is on line one, Mr. Fitzpatrick. When you pick it up, there will be a slight background noise. That's just the sound of the scrambler."

"I know, Susan, I've done this before." He pressed line one and waited. A moment later he heard the familiar voice.

"Hi, Michael. I'm sorry to keep you up so late. It's got to be three o'clock in the morning for you?"

"Good afternoon, Mr. President."

"All right, bring me up to speed. Have you been able to work out a solution for our friend?"

"Actually, sir, I think she has worked it out for herself. She indicated that she found the perfect candidate."

"Do we know who it is?"

"It turns out that he's a friend of yours, sir." Michael allowed himself a silent smile.

"Really? Who is it?"

"Joe Wilder."

"You're kidding. He's a businessman, for God's sake—an old one at that!" The president laughed. "I mean, granted, he's made a lot of money and he's a good businessman, but can he handle this kind of job?"

"You forget, sir, he parlayed eleven bodybuilding titles into a billion-dollar international company."

"I know, but we're talking about something far more dangerous than figuring out an exercise routine. If this thing goes bad, we'll need a field agent, not a negotiator."

"Well, sir, it turns out that Mr. Wilder did some work for the agency years ago. Actually, he's a very well-trained field agent."

"You're kidding." There was a moment of silence before the president continued. "Do you think he could actually pull this off?"

"He was very effective when he worked for us. Until the Paris mess, he was one of our best agents."

"What Paris mess?"

"He went shopping in Paris and walked into a department store just after a group of terrorists had killed two security guards and taken ten school children hostage. Before the police arrived, he took out three of the terrorists and rescued nine of the kids."

"What about the last child?"

"The terrorists shot a twelve-year-old boy before Wilder could get to them." Michael was quiet for a moment. "He took it very personally and blamed himself for the boy's death."

"Is that when he quit the agency?" the president asked.

"Yes, sir."

There was silence on the line for a long moment before the president spoke again.

"I just don't know. Are you sure we're doing the right thing by letting her make this decision?"

"Mr. President, we can't be more directly involved at this point in time without creating an international mess," Michael said. "This has to be her choice."

"I'm sure you're right. As you say, it's her call—but Joe Wilder? It's hard to believe he was that good." The president paused for a moment and then changed the subject. "Were you able to find out anything more about this White Wolf group?"

"We did have an informant inside the organization, but I'm afraid that has turned sour."

"What happened?"

"He was found this morning in one of the hutongs—that's one of the old neighborhoods—south of the Drum Tower. They cut his throat."

"I'm sorry." Then, almost as an afterthought, he asked whether the man could be traced back to Fitzpatrick.

"No, sir, it was a completely blind contact. He didn't even know he was working for us."

"Anything else I should know?"

"There is one more thing, Mr. President."

"Yes?"

"There might be another player involved."

"What do you mean?"

"There have been rumors of one of the old Tongs nosing around. It's a faction of the Tiandihui Tong with ties to organized crime in China dating back to the 1700s. As far as we can tell, they don't know about our friend yet."

"Does she know about them?"

"Yes, sir."

"Have you briefed the ambassador?"

"I only gave him an overview, but no details yet."

"Very well, Michael. Please keep me informed as things progress."

"Have a good afternoon, Mr. President."

THE LITTLE SMART CAR JUMPED THE RED LIGHT, CROSSED THE intersection from Valley Vista Drive, and quickly merged with the line of cars climbing the hill on Beverly Glen. Phil Banks checked his watch for the tenth time since leaving his house. It was barely six thirty, and the morning traffic from the valley into the city was already building. If he'd just gotten out of the house fifteen minutes sooner, it would have been all right. Now, the flow of traffic was barely doing twenty-five miles an hour up the hill. His blood pressure was climbing faster than the line of cars. In another mile, Beverly Glen widened into two lanes going south, and then he could make up some time.

"Just relax," he said to himself. "It won't change anything one way or the other if I'm ten minutes late."

At forty-six years of age, Phil Banks was the newest member of the Wilder Enterprises Board of Directors. This was his meeting, called to deal with their supply line crises. With any luck, he would still be on the board and still have a job after the meeting. It had been exactly three years ago today that Joe Wilder had personally given him the promotion.

His office had been nothing more than a six-foot-square partitioned cubicle on the lower floors of the Wilder Enterprises International corporate offices.

"Hey, Phil, you got a quick minute?" Joe had just sort of leaned into the area without really coming into the cubicle.

"Yes, sir." Phil had turned his chair to face the boss and gotten to his feet.

"We just had a board meeting, and you were picked to take over as VP of product development and production." He'd said it easily, as if it were something trivial. Stunned, Phil hadn't been sure he'd heard the man correctly.

"Millie will come by to see you a little later today to get you squared away. The new job comes with an office upstairs and a big pay raise. So, congratulations." Before Phil had been able to respond, Joe had smiled and disappeared.

The new job had come with a new secretary and an enormous increase in his workload, as well as a seat on the board. As it turned out, his secretary had been the best part of the deal.

Her first day on the job, Chrissie Thorn had worn a tailored business suit with a tight skirt and top that accentuated her incredible figure. She was strikingly tall even without five-inch stiletto heels. She had flaming red hair, a smile that would melt Scrooge's heart, and enough charm to be in politics.

"Good mornin', and welcome to the executive floor." The slight southern accent had added a little extra allure to the overall image. Smiling warmly, she'd leaned across his desk to place a cup of coffee in front of him, giving Phil a close up view of her ample cleavage. "Now, should I call you Phil or Mr. Banks?"

"I'm as new to this executive business as you are so suit yourself." He'd returned her smile. "And thanks for the coffee."

"Okay, Phil it is." She'd turned toward the door, but stopped short. "There are a couple of things I think you oughta know about me right off. I'm twenty-six years old and came out here from Lubbock, Texas, four months ago. I figure to give it a year to be a movie star or get married. So, this job might be a little on the short side, you know?"

"How's the movie star thing working out?" Phil had tried not to laugh.

"Well, Phil, I'm your secretary, aren't I?" Chrissie had smiled again, closing the door behind her.

They had been married six months later in a small ceremony on the beach in Malibu. Joe Wilder had given the bride away. As a wedding present to herself, Chrissie had made certain that Phil would never again have a female secretary. For their first anniversary, Phil had bought a house in Sherman Oaks. And, now, because of that drive over the hill, he was going to be late for the meeting.

He left the little car in front of the WEI Building in the only vacant space on the street, ignoring the passenger-loading-zone signs. He didn't want to waste more time fumbling for his key card at the garage entrance. Grabbing an armload of documents, he hurried toward the entrance.

The open atrium of the Wilder Building soared twelve stories above the polished granite floors of the lobby. Visitors, tenants, and employees all passed through a combination reception/security desk before turning to the elevators on either side of the atrium.

"Morning, Mr. Banks." Sam Knox, the senior of the three security officers on duty, smiled and checked the time before buzzing Phil into the lobby.

"Hi, Sam, is Mr. Wilder here yet?"

"Not yet."

"Great." He tossed his car keys to the security guard. "Could you ask one of your guys to run my car down to the garage?"

"Sure." Phil could feel Sam watching as he juggled several stacks of computer printouts while waiting for the elevator.

THE EXECUTIVE OFFICES OF WILDER ENTERPRISES INTERNATIONAL, WEI, occupied the top two floors of the building. Most of the twelfth was devoted to Joe Wilder's private office, the executive dining room, two conference rooms, and ten additional offices for various company executives. The twelfth-floor lobby was a mixture of elegance and marketing. Apart from the receptionist's desk, there were three separate sitting areas all marked by modern chrome and leather chairs scattered atop three beautiful antique Chinese carpets. More than a dozen life-size bronze sculptures of ancient Greek Olympians stood around the perimeter of the room. While each sculpture represented a different Olympic event, the central figure in the collection was a smiling likeness of Joe Wilder, arms raised in triumph and welcome, celebrating his seventh Mr. Universe win.

Visitors to the corporate offices were never quite certain if the sculptures were there for effect or as an expression of the founder's ego. In reality, Joe had learned early on to use his personality, reputation, and successes as a negotiating tool. Anyone coming through the executive lobby to deal with WEI would have to run the gauntlet of sculptures. It was an intimidating home-court advantage.

Entering the glass-enclosed conference room, Joe muttered a half-hearted good morning to the ten men and women seated around the table.

"Okay, Phil, it's your meeting. Just how bad is this situation?" Joe Wilder took his seat at the far end of the table. At sixty-four years of age, he still had the solid physique that had earned him seven Mr. Universe and six Mr. Olympia titles. The hair was a light brown, wavy with a tinge of gray, but he always maintained that he was happy just to have hair. His face was still ruggedly handsome. A warm smile and easy charm were assets he used to his advantage.

Through the years, Joe was able to turn a reputation as a savvy and winning body builder into a billion-dollar conglomerate founded on concepts of good health and exercise. Wilder Enterprises International supplied high-quality exercise equipment, free weights, weight-training machines, health foods, and nutritional supplements around the world. Wilder Fitness Centers provided members with the facilities and training to improve their own levels of fitness and good health. Through its publishing division, Wilder Publishing, WEI produced ten monthly magazines devoted to bodybuilding, exercise, health, nutrition, and fitness. By way of giving back to the community, the Wilder School Initiative provided physical fitness and healthy nutritional educational programs to schools across the country without charge. For Joe, the idea of good health and physical strength gave children a boost toward a successful long life.

"It's both bad and good." Phil passed the computerized reports down both sides of the conference table. "Our current contracts with Guangdong Light Industrial Products and their subsidiaries expires tonight at midnight. We began negotiating new contracts three months ago, but we've run into a stumbling block."

"What does that mean?" Joe asked, ignoring the printout. He knew full well that losing two-thirds of their supply chain would cripple negotiations to take WEI public in October.

"Wen Shu Xian is the deputy minister of trade for the Guangdong province in China. She oversees all of the factories that we deal with, and she has to approve all of our contracts. Initially, she demanded a thirty percent price increase in order to renew our contracts."

"That's ridiculous!" the vice president of marketing said. "No company could absorb that kind of cost increase and stay in business."

"Agreed," Phil continued. "We tried to negotiate smaller increases, even going for the thirty percent over a ten-year period, but we got turned down every time."

"Linda, how much business do we do with these people?" Joe asked.

"I thought you would ask me that." Linda Moore passed around her own thick sets of computerized reports. As controller of WEI, she had the uncanny ability to instantly put her finger on whatever financial data was needed at any given moment. Indicating the last page of the financial summaries, Linda pointed out that Guangdong Light Industrial Products supplies eighty-seven percent of the bodybuilding equipment that WEI sells.

"Although the bulk of our revenues come from the publishing, health food, vitamin supplements, and fitness-center divisions, Wilder Health and Fitness Equipment represents forty-five percent of our total gross sales. That equates to a little more than six hundred and fifty million dollars. In the last eight years, we have tripled the amount of product we buy from Guangdong Light and their subsidiaries. And, I might add, increased our bottom line net profit considerably in the process."

"There is something else to consider," Phil interjected. "The two factories supplying our health food and vitamin supplements also come under the same contracts."

"All right, we're being blackmailed," Joe stated. "Why do we have to stand for it? How long would it take us to find another factory to make these items? Can we shift the manufacturing to Indonesia or Pakistan or anyplace else?"

"Not really. The startup costs would be severe, not to mention the time delay. It would take months for us to tool up for production in another country. As it stands today, we have slightly less than a ninety-day supply of products in our US distribution centers."

"Merde!" Joe muttered. "Linda, what happens to our IPO if we need six months to retool in another country?"

"Best-case scenario is that we have to push back the initial stock offering to the end of the year. But there would also be the possibility of losing our underwriting altogether."

"If this is the bad news, what's the good?" Joe seemed to slump down into his chair.

"Well"—Phil smiled for the first time since the meeting began—"it seems that Wen Shu Xian is willing to be reasonable but only if you are willing to meet with her at the Chinese International Import and Export Fair in Guangzhou. The fair opens April 15, the day after tomorrow."

"What do you mean?"

"She told Paul Chiu in Hong Kong that she would only negotiate with you, personally, face-to-face at the fair."

Joe Wilder sat silently for a moment. Then, turning to his secretary, he asked, "Millie, can you get me on a flight to Guangzhou?"

"You are booked on Cathay Pacific out of LAX at 1:15 in the morning. The limo will be at your house at ten. You arrive in Hong Kong at 7:05 Thursday morning." She handed him the airline tickets.

"Can't I fly direct to Guangzhou?"

"You have to stay overnight in Hong Kong to get a visa for China." Millie handed him a printed itinerary. "You're booked into the Peninsula Hotel. Do you remember Maurice Chan, the general manager? He offered to send a car to the airport to pick you up. Paul will meet you for breakfast when you check in and take care of the visa. I also made a reservation for you at the White Swan Hotel in Guangzhou. You can either fly or take the train from Hong Kong."

"I'll take the train. Please let Paul know that he's coming with me. That will give him enough time to bring me up to speed on our dragon lady! Do I have copies of the last contracts to take with me?"

"I put copies in your briefcase." She put it on the table.

Joe surveyed his executive board with a sour expression on his face.

"Okay," he finally said, sitting up straight. "I guess I'm off to China."

JOE SPENT THE REST OF THE DAY IN HIS OFFICE. ASIDE FROM THE routine tasks of running a business the size of WEI, he needed to clear his calendar for the next ten days to allow for the unforeseen trip. Without Millie's organizational skills, he would have been totally lost.

"We have a photo shoot for the *Women's Fitness* cover scheduled for Friday morning." Millie said. "What do you want to do about it?"

"Can we push it off until I get back?"

"I don't think so. It took Steve a year to get Angelina to commit to do the cover. Who knows what her timetable will be if we have to reschedule."

"Shit!" Joe leaned his desk chair back and rubbed his eyes. In thirty-five years of publishing, there had never been a cover he hadn't personally supervised. "Tell Steve to make sure the shoot goes well. And tell him that if he screws up this cover, I'll break his knees!"

"Okay, I'm sure he'll be thrilled with the assignment." Millie smiled at the meaningless threat. "The only things left on the list are your dinner date Saturday night and the Cystic Fibrosis fund-raiser on Sunday."

"Can you call Helen at the CF Foundation and explain what we're up against? Tell her I'll send a check before I leave." Joe sat up and reached for his rolodex. "I'll call Sherri and cancel dinner."

At five o'clock, Joe stood in the middle of his office, briefcase in hand, almost ready to leave but with a quizzical expression on his face.

"If you've forgotten anything, you can always send me an email." She was quiet for a moment. Joe noticed the obvious concerned expression.

"What's wrong, Millie?

"I was just wondering if this mess could have anything to do with your past."

"Not a chance!" His expression changed to a warm smile as he gave her a hug. "Don't worry. This is just business. I'll call you when I get to Hong Kong."

And, with that said, he straightened up and walked out the door. He smiled again and waved as the elevator doors closed. Joe always considered hiring Millie Grant the best business decision he'd ever made. She had become his first employee at the age of twenty-four, fresh out of college with a liberal arts degree, long blond hair that hung down to her waist and a killer figure. Over the last thirty-five years she became his secretary, confidant, personal assistant and friend. They had seen each other through love affairs—both bad and good—marriages, divorces and, in her case, widowhood. Joe appreciated the fact that she felt it was one of the perks of her job to worry about the boss. And he was grateful that she did it so very well. In some small measure, she made up for his lack of family.

THROUGHOUT HIS YEARS AS A COMPETITOR AND LATER AS A businessman, Joe had logged hundreds of thousands of miles flying around the world. The main lessons learned were to take as little luggage as possible and that it was usually impossible to sleep on long overseas flights. As a result, Joe had developed his own routine for in-flight survival.

Cathay Pacific Flight 881 from Los Angeles to Hong Kong would be a grueling fifteen hours. Even in first class with a wide selection of movies, videogames, multiple meals, and smiling, shapely flight attendants as distractions, it was too many hours to be confined in an airplane seat. In theory, Joe reasoned, a traveler should arrive early enough to avoid the longer last-minute check-in lines. In spite of the late departure time, Joe decided to skip dinner. From experience, he knew Cathay Pacific would start serving drinks and snacks immediately after takeoff, with dinner following an hour later. Once in China, he would need to work out an extra hour each day for the rest of the trip in order to lose the weight gain from the flight.

With more than two hours to spare, Joe checked in at the Cathay Pacific counter and then moved on to the first-class-priority security checkpoint. His luggage for this trip was sparse, consisting of a folding garment bag and a wheeled carry-on. Security let the garment bag through without comment, but he was still required to remove his laptop, belt, and shoes. The whole thing took less than twenty minutes.

Boarding pass in hand, Joe took his time walking down the hall toward the Cathay Pacific Airlines gate. Passing a number of restaurants, bars, and duty-free shops, he headed directly to the Hudson News stand. It was a fairly large shop for an airport, offering books, both paperbacks and hard cover, as well as various sundries, cosmetics, snacks, and some fifteen feet of magazines and international newspapers. Whenever he traveled, Joe took the time to check the positioning of each one of Wilder Enterprises publications. As with any product, placement on a store shelf or counter equated to sales—or the lack thereof. He was pleased to see that his ten current issues were displayed prominently in the racks as well as next to the checkout stands. Smiling with a tinge of parental pride, Joe left the store without a purchase and turned down the hall again toward his gate.

He found a seat near the podium and spent the next half hour sorting through some correspondence and responding to several last-minute emails on his laptop. Gradually, the area began filling with passengers. Some found seats around or near the podium, while others stood in line by the door leading to the Jetway. Without making a conscious effort, Joe took note of the other passengers. They were a fairly eclectic mix of business people heading to the Canton Fair and tourists eager to see the sights. And, as expected, the flight was sold out.

"Ladies and gentlemen, at this time, we would like to board our first-class and priority-club passengers." A Cathay Pacific gate attendant stood by the door, waiting to tear their boarding passes. Joe moved down the Jetway and was greeted by a stewardess when he stepped on board.

"Welcome aboard, Mr. Wilder," she said, checking his boarding pass. "You are in 3F. That's on the far side of the plane. Would you like me to hang your garment bag?"

"Yes, thank you." *One less thing to deal with*, he thought.

Millie had reserved a window seat in the third row of the first-class cabin. The seating was configured with rows of six seats across—a window and aisle seat on each side of the plane and a center section of two seats. Although lacking the new cocoon like pods of the newer planes, the seats were comfortably wide, capable of fully reclining and separated by a large console. Joe began to wonder if it might be possible to sleep on this flight after all.

After stowing the carry-on bag in the overhead bin along with his jacket, Joe settled into his seat and began a last-minute text message to Millie as the remaining passengers streamed into the plane crowding the aisles. A young man dropped his carry-on and briefcase in the aisle seat one row in front of Joe and then turned to his companion.

"You're in 3E, so it looks like we're going to be separated for the duration." Leaning over the back of his seat, he addressed Joe. "Excuse me, but would you be willing to trade seats with me?"

Joe glanced at the young woman standing in the aisle. He had noticed the couple when they'd arrived at the gate. They seemed particularly out of place among the three hundred or so passengers waiting for the flight. Late, out of breath and running, they'd reached the podium just as the gate agents began to board passengers. Probably in his early thirties, the young man wore a dark, well-tailored business suit with his tie pulled loose. Also in her early thirties and attractive, the young woman was similarly dressed in a business suit. While they were together, they didn't seem to be a couple. It was that very discordant note that caught Joe's attention. They looked exactly like lawyers going to or coming from a settlement conference. Joe had seen their type in hundreds of business meetings through the years, but they did not look like business people embarking on a fifteen-hour overseas flight.

"No!" She silently mouthed her plea from behind her companion.

"Sorry," Joe replied with a smile, "I get car sick on long trips if I don't sit next to an open window."

"Funny." The younger man was not amused, but turned around to settle into his seat, leaving the young woman to deal with the overhead bin unassisted. Once seated, she turned to Joe and extended her hand.

"I'm Cathy Martin, thanks for the help." She smacked the top of the seat in front of her. "This hunk of bad manners is my associate Tim Roberts." The young man raised his arm above the seat back and waved.

"It was a pleasure." He shook her hand and then turned his attention back to the unfinished text. At the same time, he surreptitiously snapped a photo of the young woman and added it to the message. "I take it you aren't that fond of your traveling partner."

"He's okay, I guess." She paused thoughtfully for a moment then continued. "He just gets very intense, too intense. The idea of sitting next to him all the way to Hong Kong was not very appealing. I hope that's all right?"

"It's okay with me." Joe smiled again. "I'm Joe Wilder, by the way."

"I know. We actually met last year at the children's hospital fundraiser." They spent the next few minutes comparing mutual acquaintances and friends in common.

"Are you going to Hong Kong for business or pleasure?" Joe asked.

"Pure business, we're actually going to the fair." She nodded toward the young man seated in front of her. "Tim and I work for the Disney Company."

"Really?" Joe seemed surprised. "To be honest, I thought you were both lawyers with the Securities and Exchange Commission."

"Oh God, no! Are we that obvious?" She laughed. "We're in-house counsel doing the product and character-trademark licensing for the company. Another group was supposed to make this trip, but something came up at the last minute, and we got the call at one this afternoon."

The stewardess brought them glasses of champagne. They sipped the wine and continued to get acquainted. While Cathy seemed perfectly happy to ignore her traveling companion, Joe managed to finish the text message to Millie between snippets of conversation. Less than twenty minutes later, the doors were closed and the big Boeing 777 was pushed back from the gate and began to taxi toward the runway.

"Ladies and gentlemen this is your captain speaking. I'd like to welcome you aboard Cathay Pacific Flight 881 to Hong Kong. It looks like a great night for flying. We have clear skies, a full moon and twenty miles of visibility. Our flying time should be about fourteen hours and twenty-seven minutes. So, sit back, relax, and have a pleasant flight."

As the giant plane revved her engines on the runway apron, the interior cabin lights were dimmed.

"What happened to the lights?" Cathy asked. She sounded like a frightened little girl.

"You have a better view of the city lights as we take off if the cabin is dark."

A moment later, the brakes were released, and the giant plane lumbered down the runway gathering speed. As if in slow motion, they lifted off the runway and began a steep climb over Dockweiler beach and out over Santa Monica Bay.

"Exactly 1:15," Joe said softly.

"I guess that's a good thing, right?" Cathy asked.

"Is this your first trip to Hong Kong?"

"Well," she still seemed nervous, "it's my first trip outside the US."

"Don't worry. It'll be fine," he said and smiled. "You'll love it! If you can, spend a few days in Hong Kong either before or after the fair."

"Sure." She closed her eyes and swallowed hard as the plane banked to the right.

Looking out the window, Joe watched the lights of Santa Monica Pier and the city recede into the distance quickly becoming small points in the darkness. Their flight path took them north along the coast as they continued to climb to their cruising altitude of thirty-six thousand feet. Once at their altitude, the cabin lights came back on, and the crew began to prepare for the meal.

"Ladies and gentlemen, the captain has turned off the seat belt sign so feel free to move about the cabin. We will begin our beverage service shortly."

Once their champagne glasses had been refilled for the third time, Cathy seemed to recover some of her earlier spirit.

"Are you feeling better?" Joe asked.

"Yes, thanks." She smiled again. "I'm not a great flyer. The truth is it scares the hell out of me. Takeoff and landings are the worst!"

They spent the next four hours discussing everything from business to religion and politics. It was get-to-know-you conversation over a pair of perfectly prepared steaks and an excellent California cabernet. By the time their ice cream sundaes were a sweet memory, Joe felt like he'd just been on a first date.

"Tell me more about Hong Kong?" Cathy asked.

"It's an incredible city. One that has to be experienced not just talked about."

"For example?" There was a teasing tone in her voice.

"Okay, where are you staying?"

"We're at the Holiday Inn, but only for one night. We have to get visas for China. Then we're off to Guangzhou." She butchered the pronunciation.

"It's a great location on Nathan Road. You can walk to the Star Ferry or take the MTR over to Hong Kong. On the Hong Kong side, you take the tram to the top of Victoria Peak. The view is incredible. Then you have to visit Repulse Bay and have dinner on the Floating Restaurant. The Kowloon side has some of the best shopping in the world. There are big name boutiques all along Nathan Road. And then there is this thing called the Ladies' Market. Blocks and blocks of streets closed to vehicles.

Hundreds of small stands fill the boulevards with anything you could possibly want to buy. Now that's an experience!"

"But we only have one day!" She seemed awestruck.

"What about after the fair?"

"I don't really know if we can take a couple of days off on our way home." She seemed to be trying to think of a way to make it happen.

Finally, Tim stood in the aisle and stretched. Opening the overhead bin, he retrieved his briefcase and removed a thick file folder. Leaning over Cathy's seat, he dropped it on her tray table.

"Can you take some time now and look over these contracts?"

She gave him a withering look before opening the file.

"I think that's my cue to take a walk." Joe squeezed past them and began walking the aisles of the airplane. The stewardess smiled, but wouldn't let him wander past the business-class section. By the time he'd finished his third-round trip, Joe found Cathy studiously working her way through a thick stack of documents. Tim had withdrawn to his own seat without further comment.

"Don't mind me. I'm going to try and get some sleep." Joe slipped back into his seat and pushed the control buttons that extended the leg rests and footrests while reclining his seat nearly flat. Reaching over to the console, he turned off the reading light and stuck a pillow under his neck. To no one's surprise but his own, Joe was sound asleep within minutes.

WHEN HE OPENED HIS EYES AGAIN, MOST OF THE CABIN WAS IN darkness. Only one or two reading lights were lit, and just one personal video screen seemed to be in use. The constant hum of the engines had a slightly hypnotic effect and easily lulled already tired passengers to sleep. Glancing at his watch, Joe realized he had slept for nearly six hours. That was a first. He couldn't remember the last time he'd slept on an overseas flight. Raising the window shade, he saw the sky around them beginning to turn gray.

Another hour, he thought, *and we'll catch up to the sunrise.*

With less than three hours of flight time remaining, the cabin crew turned on the lights and began their morning routine prior to landing. Although it smelled tempting, Joe declined breakfast, choosing orange juice and coffee instead.

"Are you sure?" Cathy asked. "This cheese omelet is really pretty good for airline food."

Sometime during the night, she had changed into cotton slacks, a sweater set, and flat shoes. She looked fresh and rested.

"I'm meeting someone for breakfast when we land."

The crew worked with smooth efficiency, clearing the dishes and food carts from the aisles just as the captain announced their descent into Hong Kong International Airport.

Joe stared out of the window as they broke through the cloud cover over Hong Kong. Long sweeping views of the Hong Kong harbor, a sea of high-rise buildings that lined the water's edge, and countless small islands dotting the area gave way to an impressive view of the man-made island that was the new international airport. Joe thought back to his first flights into the old Hong Kong International Airport years before. It was always a slow descent through the clouds until the buildings of Kowloon seemed to rush up to the plane. A sharp right turn followed by an immediate steep dive brought the plane down on the runway with a bone-jarring thud.

"It's like landing a 777 on a postage stamp!" A pilot once explained to Joe. "Down fast and stop short. And try not to slide into the harbor."

The glide path into the new airport was a long, slow descent that afforded passengers a breathtaking panoramic view of Hong Kong Island, Kowloon and the nearly three hundred small islands that made up the former crown colony.

"It's so beautiful!" Cathy said as they passed over several small islands. Her fear of flying seemed to have vanished for the moment.

The plane banked again as the pilot started their final approach. A few minutes later, a gentle bump and the muffled roar of the engines reversing thrust was the only indication that they had actually landed.

"Ladies and gentlemen, welcome to Hong Kong where the local time is seven fifteen in the morning. The weather forecast is for sunny skies and a high of twenty-five Centigrade, seventy-seven Fahrenheit. We hope you enjoy your stay in Hong Kong!"

Once the ground crew had opened the door, Joe bid a quick farewell to Cathy and her associate, slipped on his jacket, and made a hasty exit down the Jetway. At this hour of the morning, there would be any number of flights arriving from various cities around the world. Even with the efficiency of the new airport, he reasoned, the rush would cause delays at passport control. With only a carry-on and garment bag, once through immigration, Joe could bypass the baggage-claim area altogether.

"You have visited Hong Kong many times, Mr. Wilder?" The immigration officer asked as he flipped through Joe's passport, looking for a blank spot to stamp the entry. There were years when he traveled to China every other month. The State Department added extra pages to his passports in order to accommodate the visa entries.

"It's been a while," Joe replied as the officer stamped his passport and handed it back.

"Welcome to Hong Kong."

He followed the green Nothing-to-Declare line out of customs to avoid unnecessary delays. The last set of automatic doors opened to the airport lobby where a sizeable crowd waited for arriving passengers. They were separated by a chest high railing that ran parallel to the wall and opened at either end. Toward the back of the crowd, Joe spotted a young man holding a sign bearing Joe's name. He was in his early twenties and wore the distinctive green blazer of the Peninsula Hotel. Joe worked his way through the crowd and approached the young man from behind.

"Are you looking for me?"

"Ah, yes, Mr. Wilder?" He seemed a little startled. "I did not see you. I am here to drive you to hotel. May I have your luggage claim check?"

"No luggage, just what I have in my hands."

"Allow me, sir." He quickly took the carry-on and garment bag. "If you please follow me, the car is this way."

A new Rolls-Royce Phantom, painted that same Peninsula Green, was parked unattended just outside the terminal exit. Once the two bags were loaded into the boot, the elegant car was moving out of the airport toward the city.

"My Western name is Nixon, Mr. Wilder." The young man smiled broadly in the rearview mirror. He spoke excellent English with just a trace of a British accent. "I am to be your driver while you are at the Peninsula."

"That's quite a name."

"My parents said he was a great American president. Everyone in China has a Chinese name and a Western name. I think it would not be possible for you to say my Chinese name." He pronounced something unintelligible and smiled.

"Fair enough, Nixon, whatever you say." He returned the young man's smile. "Are you from Hong Kong? You speak excellent English."

"No, sir, I'm from Shenzhen, but I grew up here. Sir, would you like me to take the tunnel into the city, or do you prefer the views from the bridge on the upper roads?"

"Just take the fastest route possible. I have a meeting at the hotel as soon as we arrive."

"Very well, sir."

The traffic was fairly light by Hong Kong standards, and they seemed to make good time. Driving out of the airport complex, they quickly merged with the traffic on the Lantau Highway. Five minutes into their drive, Joe's cell phone rang.

"Good evening, Millie." He was expecting her call. She always checked to see that he had arrived safely. It had become a ritual of their relationship through the years.

"And a good morning to you too! How was your flight?"

"The flight was good—I actually slept on the plane."

"I'm surprised, given your pretty traveling companion. How the hell did you manage to get that photograph?"

"I was in the middle of sending you a text when she settled into the seat next to me. Did you find out anything?"

"I checked with Rachel at children's hospital. There was no one named Cathy Martin or Tim Roberts on the guest list for the event last year. And they're not on the list for this year either. But that doesn't prove anything one way or the other."

"I know. She could have been someone's date or a guest of one of the donors."

"What do you want me to do?" Millie asked.

"Check with one of our contacts at Disney. I'd like to know for sure, one way or the other."

"Okay." Millie paused for a moment. "Joe, I thought you said this has nothing to do with the past?"

"It doesn't. But the fact that we're in the middle of a crisis with our supplier that's forced me to come to China makes me just a little bit curious." He paused for a moment. "I'm sorry, Millie. There's just something about her story that didn't match the image of the two people I saw on the plane. I want to make sure that rumors of our problems haven't given the SEC jitters."

"You know"—she paused again, this time for effect—"it could just be that you're still a good-looking guy and she felt like being friendly!"

"Thanks for the compliment." He smiled into the phone. "I'll call you tomorrow."

JOE NEVER NOTICED THE OLDER EUROPEAN COUPLE AT THE AIRPORT. They were standing off to one side near the Hong Kong Tourist Bureau display. Waiting patiently, the couple watched as the young man in the green blazer held up a sign each time a group of passengers came through the customs doorway. When he finally found his passenger, they followed at a discreet distance observing the young driver load the luggage into the boot of the Rolls-Royce. They remained unnoticed, climbing into a waiting taxicab and followed the big car out of the airport.

Neither driver nor passenger noticed the taxicab following behind the Rolls. Unlike the dozens of taxis on the highway, it appeared to match their speed, never getting closer but never falling back either. It might have seemed curious to a casual observer, but no one noticed. Two more minutes and the Rolls reached the Tsing Ma Bridge, the seventh largest suspension bridge in the world.

The traffic on the bridge seemed fairly light by Hong Kong standards. Either they had beaten the morning rush, or it was yet to begin. At the crest of the bridge, Joe looked off to the right as he'd done on so many earlier trips. From that vantage point, the view of Victoria Harbor with Hong Kong and Kowloon in the distance was breathtaking. It took the big Rolls another five minutes to cross over the bridge and get stuck in the heavier congestion of the Kowloon Expressway.

"Can you get us out of this traffic?" Joe asked.

"We better use city streets now, I think," Nixon commented as he guided the Phantom off the highway. He found an opening and maneuvered across two lanes of traffic to the off ramp.

Once down on the street level, he turned the big car away from the Kowloon freight terminals, sliding through traffic and negotiating the narrow streets with ease. After driving on Canton Road for half a mile, they made the transition to Kowloon Park Drive. From there, it took less than a minute to make the turn on to Salisbury Road. Joe could see the Peninsula Hotel three blocks away.

"On the left side is the YMCA building." Nixon gave him a running commentary on the buildings as they past. "That big round dome is the Hong Kong Space Museum and our Museum of Fine Art is right behind. You like art? The German expressionist exhibition now is supposed to be very good."

"Thank you," Joe said simply, not wanting to ruin his moment.

As the Rolls-Royce Phantom turned into the driveway and came around the fountain to the main entrance of the Peninsula Hotel, Joe was treated to the full effect of the elegant facade and arched entry of the grand old building. The combination of classical architecture and meticulously designed staff uniforms was meant to welcome and impress new arrivals. When it was built in 1928, it was intended to be the most luxurious hotel east of Suez. At the time, the eastern terminus of the Orient Express Trans-Siberian railroad was the Kowloon station, only two blocks from the hotel. Passenger liners from around the world docked just across Salisbury Road, where the art and space museums now stand. Then, as now, the Peninsula Hotel was *the* place to stay.

"Good morning and welcome to the Peninsula." The uniformed doorman held the car door open while a bellman retrieved the luggage.

"Good morning, sir, do you have a reservation?" A young woman, whose nameplate read Janice, was at the desk. She smiled graciously as Joe handed over his passport.

"Oh, yes, Mr. Wilder. Our general manager has been expecting you."

Without waiting for a reply, she lifted the telephone receiver and dialed an extension. In an instant, Maurice Chan appeared beside her. He was in his late fifties, carrying thirty pounds too much weight for his height—a testament to his love of French cooking, inherited from his mother, and his disdain for exercise.

"Joe, my old friend, it is so good to see you!" Coming around the desk, he gripped Joe's hand, pumping it vigorously. "I was so happy to get Millie's call that you were coming. Everything is arranged. I have a suite waiting for you with a view of the harbor."

"Thank you, Maurice, it's good to see you again. And thanks for sending the car to the airport."

The two had first met thirty-five years ago when Joe had begun importing from mainland China. In those early years, the only way to get to the fair had been by train from Kowloon, thus requiring an overnight stay. On that first buying trip, Joe had been stressed, still on Los Angeles time and in need of a workout. The constant clanking of the metal weights had echoed through the lower levels of the basement and aroused Maurice's curiosity. He'd left the handcart loaded with wine in the freight elevator and followed the sound. He'd found Joe in the hotel gym sweating away his stress. From that moment on, they had remained good friends.

"It is my pleasure. Nixon will be available for you as long as you're here." He went back around the desk. "Janice will have your luggage taken up to your suite. But for now, your friend Paul is waiting for you in the lobby restaurant." He handed Joe a small envelope containing his electronic room key.

"Thanks again, Maurice. Maybe we can have a drink later and catch up on the last few years?"

"I would like that my friend."

By design, the lobby of the Peninsula Hotel was an invitation to travel back in time to the halcyon days of the British crown colony. Beautiful fresh flowers, potted palms, and ferns were scattered everywhere. Neoclassical arches supported the coffered ceiling that soared thirty-five feet above a black-and-white-marble floor. The intricate carvings that graced the tops of the many columns supporting the ceiling were gilded in twenty-four-karat gold leaf. At the time of construction, teams of artists, specialists in the art of restoring the carved altar pieces in the churches of Rome, had been brought from Italy to create the beautiful carved figures and moldings to decorate the walls and ceiling.

A string quartet performed daily from a small balcony overlooking the lobby. Every afternoon, the lobby restaurant served a traditional English high tea, complete with finger sandwiches, scones, clotted cream, and an array of tempting pastries. Through the years, afternoon tea has become a *must-do* experience when visiting Hong Kong. It was said that more business deals were consummated during high tea at the Peninsula than in all the board rooms of Hong Kong. But then again, that might have been an exaggeration.

Joe found his old friend sitting alone at a table for four just opposite the wide staircase leading to the mezzanine shops. Although Paul Chiu was well into his fifties, he had a full head of thick, black hair just beginning to show a little gray. He had an unlined, youthful face and was quick with an ever-ready warm smile. Born and raised in Taipei, Paul had started a small manufacturing-and-trading company thirty-five years earlier when his former employer had gone bankrupt. His first customer was Joe Wilder. The two men had become good friends over the years.

"How long have you been nursing that pot of tea?" Joe asked, as he pulled out a chair and sat down.

"It's been cold for about an hour." Paul smiled and reached across the table to shake hands. "Good to see you, Joe. How was your flight?"

"Are you hungry? I'm starved. Can we order breakfast?" Joe ignored the question. "How are Janet and the kids?"

"Sure. It's only eight thirty in the morning." Paul signaled the waiter. "And my family is fine. Thanks for asking."

After ordering two cheddar cheese omelets, crisp bacon, fresh fruit, bran muffins, and a pot of coffee, the two men finally focused on the business at hand.

"The first thing we have to do this morning is get you a visa. It will cost extra, but they'll have it ready by four o'clock this afternoon."

"Where do we have to go?" Joe asked.

"Same place," Paul replied. "Around the corner, just off Nathan Road, the Chinese National Tourist Office. Do you want to come with me for the visa?"

"No, I'd appreciate it if you could take care of it for me. There are a couple of things I need to do this afternoon."

"Okay." Paul held out his hand. "Give me your passport."

"What about the train tickets?" Joe asked, handing over the document.

"I already bought two first-class tickets on the 10:00 a.m. train to Guangzhou. That means we have to be there no later than 9:00 a.m. So I'll pick you up at 8:30 tomorrow morning. They won't wait, and they won't be late."

"No problem." Joe smiled. "I just won't unpack."

"Good!" Paul said laughing. "I still remember watching you run through Kowloon Station dragging your suitcase while I was yelling at the conductor to hold the train."

"That was a terrible day!" He cringed and laughed at the memory. "My flight from LA was delayed five hours, and there were no cabs at the airport. That was the old Hong Kong International Airport. When I finally found a cab, he refused to take me to the station because it was too short a trip. I had to pay him three times the fare on the meter."

THE OLDER EUROPEAN COUPLE FROM THE AIRPORT, KNOWN SIMPLY as Sally and John, had quietly occupied a table a little distance away. From that vantage point, they watched the American and his Chinese friend. They weren't close enough to hear the conversation, but then it wasn't really necessary. Shortly after being seated, they were joined by two young men in their early twenties. Both men appeared to be lean and athletic, one was blond and Nordic looking while the other was dark haired. The dark suits they wore were stylish enough, but nothing about the two men was particularly memorable.

"Well?" If someone were actually listening to their conversation, the woman would seem to be in charge.

"I followed the bellboy up to his suite. After he left, I conned the maid into unlocking the door for me." The blonde was the younger of the two men and had a charming smile. The other young man seemed to have a perpetual sour expression.

"Did you find anything?" the older man, John, asked.

"Nothing! His carry-on wasn't even locked. If he's got anything, it has to be in his briefcase."

"What about the bug?" she asked, a sudden look of concern crossing her face.

"I put one in the night table lamp and one in his suitcase. But the range is limited. One of us has to be here, in the hotel to pick up anything." He patted the heavy briefcase sitting on the floor beside his chair. "By the way, he's checking out early in the morning."

"That's nicely done, thank you." She patted his cheek in a very grandmotherly kind of way for all the world to see. After all, perception is everything.

"Why, Sally, that's the nicest thing you've ever said to me," he replied sarcastically.

They sat and watched the two men as they finished their breakfast and paid the bill. When Joe got to his feet, Sally signaled the two young men.

"If he heads toward the elevators, just sit tight here. If he's going for the street, both of you keep tabs on him. But make sure he doesn't spot you." She took a sip of cold tea. "Unless something unexpected happens, we'll meet back here at seven thirty tomorrow morning."

They watched Joe cross the lobby toward the hotel shops. By the time he reached Nathan Road and turned left, the two young men had to hustle to keep up. Suddenly, they lost sight of him as he disappeared in the mass of humanity on the street. Moments later, they spotted him again sprinting through traffic to cross the street to the Holiday Inn. They stayed close to lessen the risk of losing him on the crowded streets of Kowloon.

EARLY THE NEXT MORNING, SALLY AND JOHN WERE WELL ENSCONCED at the same table in the lobby restaurant. They had a clear line of sight to the main entrance of the hotel, the two side entrances, and the staircase leading to the mezzanine. Within minutes, they were joined by the two young men.

"Well?" Sally asked.

"Well what?" the dark-haired man shot back. "It was pointless."

"What do you mean?" Tom asked,

"He really didn't do anything." The blonde seemed to be more relaxed about the assignment. "We followed him all day but came up empty. He was just running errands. First, he went to Wing King Optical across the street in the Holiday Inn, then some tailor at the Regent Hotel, and then back here."

"He took a workout in the gym and then had dinner with that guy Maurice Chan." The dark-haired man seemed disappointed. "Then it was back to his room for the night."

"The guy's a bore!" the blonde added as he tore a cinnamon roll in half.

"We got nothing on the tapes." Sally was annoyed. "Are you sure the bugs were working?"

She filled the young man's coffee cup from the silver pitcher a waiter had placed on the table. Glancing up, she noticed Joe crossing the lobby headed directly toward their table.

"Oh shit!" she muttered.

"Good morning." Joe stood between the two young men and addressed Sally. "Tell your employer that you owe him a refund." Reaching out with one hand, he dropped the two electronic devices in the center of the table. "If I ever see either of you tailing me again, I'll break both your legs!" He spoke softly, smiled, and then walked away, leaving them dumbstruck.

~ ✶ ~

AFTER LOADING THEIR LUGGAGE INTO THE BOOT, NIXON HEADED the green Rolls-Royce into the traffic on Salisbury Road. A quick U-turn and then right on Kowloon Park Drive had them moving at a good pace.

"It take me only twenty or twenty-five minutes to drive to the station." Nixon explained, the nervous tension in his voice was unmistakable. "But now they are building a new train station, and sometimes the traffic is very difficult."

"We're okay, Nixon. We have plenty of time before our train leaves," Joe said reassuringly.

Once the Phantom turned onto Austin Road, traffic seemed to slow to a crawl.

"You got the ten o'clock train, right?" Nixon asked.

"Yes," Paul replied. "But don't worry. It's only eight forty-five now."

Joe watched as their driver checked and adjusted the mirrors repeatedly, seeming to be searching for a gap in the traffic to accommodate the big green car.

"I know, but we are going to have trouble at the Nga Cheung Road roundabout. That is where the construction trucks block the road all the time. I hope we make it."

It was another hour before the Phantom finally pulled up in front of the station. Dozens of taxicabs, private cars, and a few hotel shuttle buses were all vying for a spot to unload their passengers. Nixon carefully maneuvered the big green car to the curb and quickly emptied the boot, loading their luggage and carry-ons onto an unused cart standing nearby.

"You got to hurry now, I think." Nixon smiled and wished them a good trip.

"Thank you, Nixon. You have been very helpful." Joe pressed several bills into the young man's hand.

"Thank you, Mr. Wilder."

Joe followed close behind as Paul deftly pushed their way through the sea of humanity that filled the main hall of Kowloon Station. Between the throngs of people on their way to the fair, the normal complement of tourists visiting Hong Kong and the locals making their daily commute, it was difficult to find a clear path to the escalators leading to the platforms.

"I don't remember it being so crowded the last time I was here," Joe commented.

"The new construction has everything messed up. You know, more people in less space. Also, the fair is much bigger now." Paul abandoned the luggage cart at the top of the escalator. "We're down one level on platform one, car number five."

"Guangzhou!" A conductor stood on the platform calling out the destination. Paul showed the tickets to a porter who took their bags and led them down the platform to their coach. Once on board, he stowed their suitcases, wished them a good trip, and graciously accepted a tip.

"My God, that was exhausting!" Joe exclaimed and laughed.

"Yeah, but we made it on time." Paul checked his watch. "And we have ten minutes to spare."

At ten o'clock precisely, with a slight lurch and two blasts of a whistle, the train began to move. A disembodied female voice asked that they pay attention to the safety video playing on the overhead monitors at the end of the coach. She repeated the request in three languages. A few minutes later, a very pretty uniformed stewardess pushed an elegant tea cart loaded with brightly packaged candies, cookies, and sweets down the aisle.

"May I offer you some tea or snacks?"

"No, thanks." Joe returned her smile before turning to his friend. "Do you want something?"

Paul simply shook his head and then reached for his briefcase to retrieve two large files. Dropping the tray tables, he spread out copies of their last contract with Guangdong Light Industrial Products Company. Joe flipped through one set of documents and then simply scowled at the stack of papers in frustration.

"You've been working with this woman for a long time, Paul. Do you have any idea what she really wants?"

"I think she has made her position very clear," Paul replied. "She insisted on a face-to-face meeting with you. So, whatever it is she wants, it's going to be up to you to figure it out."

"I guess." Joe was thoughtful for a moment, wondering how he was going to negotiate with the woman when she held all the cards.

The train emerged from the Hong Kong MTR subway tunnel system into the bright morning sunlight, increasing speed as they made their way into the New Territories. Paul flipped through the pages of their expiring contracts one after another, marking certain paragraphs with a highlighter, and then passed them to Joe, who began leafing through the first set of contracts. After a few minutes, he simply closed the folder and handed it back to Paul.

"It's pointless. You might as well put the files away," Joe said. "She is going tell us what she is willing to do for us and how much it's going to cost once we get to the fair."

Paul returned the folders to his briefcase. They sat quietly for a while, staring out the window at the passing landscape before Paul spoke again.

"I arranged for a car from the hotel to meet us at Guangzhou station. The driver will take our bags to the hotel, but I think we should go right to the fair. I think the quicker we get this meeting over with the better."

"I'm sure you're right." Joe, engrossed in thought, had turned his attention to the view from the speeding train. "How old were you the first time you came to Hong Kong?"

"My father brought me when I was six." Paul smiled at the memory. "We stayed in Kowloon with my uncle and his family. What about you?"

"I was seventeen years old and a first-time contestant in the Mr. Universe Competition." The stewardess brought two steaming cups of tea. "It was my first trip overseas, and I was scared to death."

"I can't believe that you were afraid of anything, even at seventeen."

"The organizers of the competition treated us like visiting royalty. We were taken on tours all over Hong Kong. They took us up Victoria Peak, out to the Aberdeen floating city, and out here to the New Territories. Back then, this area was mostly farmlands with a few tiny villages scattered around."

The sight of tens of thousands of shanties built from discarded trash covering the hillsides surrounding Kowloon and the New Territories had a sobering effect on the young body builder. The poverty was shocking.

"Back then my father worked for a civil engineering firm," Paul said. "His company was hired by the colonial government to design whole new cities for the Territories."

"A few months after the competition, I heard that a massive monsoon had washed away half of the shantytowns, leaving thousands of people homeless." Joe couldn't imagine how anyone had survived the onslaught.

"That's when they started pushing their New Town development," Paul commented. "My father began spending six months a year working with the colonial government."

Now, the farmlands were mostly gone, replaced by a forest of apartment buildings soaring more than a hundred stories skyward and separated by manicured parks, schoolyards, swimming pools, and athletic fields. The city itself had grown out into the New Territories at an incredible rate, fueled by unimaginable economic growth. Modern, wide boulevards carried the vehicular traffic from Kowloon to the old border checkpoint at Shenzhen and on to Guangzhou.

Before Hong Kong had been returned to China, the run from Kowloon to Guangzhou had taken a little more than three hours. At Shenzhen, the Hong Kong engine and crew were replaced with a Chinese locomotive and personnel. The new high-speed trains were far more luxurious and cut the travel time to just over two hours.

Located in the newer eastern section of the city, the new Guangzhou station was a decided improvement. While the old station seemed to have grown up in the center of the city without too much forethought, the new station was well thought-out and designed for the needs of arriving business travelers. As a result, they breezed through customs and passport control.

TWO

THE CHINA INTERNATIONAL IMPORT EXPORT FAIR, THE CANTON
Fair, is held over a period of three weeks twice a year in the spring and fall.
The Convention Center was specifically created to house the event and
consists of three buildings with a total of more than one million square feet
under roof. Everything China mines, assembles, harvests, or manufactures
is exhibited. The array of products is staggering.

As the listed agent for Wilder Enterprises International, Paul had
preregistered their names. The result was a quick check-in. With badges
hung around their necks, an exhibitor map and floor plan in hand, Joe
followed his friend as they wound their way through the crowds and
passed hundreds of small exhibitor booths in the main hall.

New cars, motorcycles, scooters, farm equipment, and oversized and
miniaturized televisions and computer screens were displayed opposite
booths offering bolts of finished silks. Each province of China seemed
to have its own section of the exhibition hall to show their wares. Near

the center of the main building, they found the five booths occupied by Guangdong Light Industrial Products.

The center booth had been set up to serve as a small conference area with four chairs, a small folding table, and a sideboard holding pots of hot tea and cups. The remaining booths were filled with samples of builders and cabinet hardware, small power tools, and high-tech electronic calibration equipment as well as examples of WEI exercise and bodybuilding equipment.

Joe stood uneasily in the aisle as Paul approached the woman seated at the small table. Leaning over slightly, he spoke to her in Chinese. A moment later, she rose, approached Joe, and extended her hand.

"I am very happy to finally meet you, Mr. Wilder." She was a little taller than Joe expected, with a slim figure and a very pretty face. Her dark hair was cut short and done in a wavy Western style. She had a warm, firm handshake. Joe guessed her age to be late forties, but he couldn't really tell.

"After doing business with Wilder Enterprises for so many years, I feel that I already know you. Thank you for accepting our invitation to come to the fair." She led him back into the booth, leaving Paul standing off to the side.

"You're welcome, but I didn't think I had too much choice."

"I guess that will depend on how our discussions go this morning, won't it?" She smiled again, but her eyes seemed guarded. "Please sit down."

Observing the ritual formality of doing business in the Orient, they sipped hot Chinese tea and exchanged business cards. The woman laughed as Joe tried in vain to pronounce her name.

"I found it much easier to use the name Wendy when I started dealing with Westerners."

"Your English is very good." As a rule, Joe had very little patience for small talk but realized the importance of this part of the custom.

"The study of English is required in China beginning in the second grade." She paused for a moment, watching him closely. "I also received my MBA at UCLA."

"Ah, that explains it." Joe flipped open his briefcase and retrieved the file Linda Moore had prepared for him. "Shall we get down to business?"

"Of course." Her gaze seemed to shift constantly, but her eyes always came back to focus on him. They were dark and penetrating one moment and sparkling with humor at some hidden joke the next.

"I have to tell you, Wendy, I'm not very happy with the way you got me here." Joe realized that she may have been smiling, but the outcome of their conversation could mean the life or death of his business.

"I can promise you, Mr. Wilder, you won't regret it." She leaned across the table to add emphasis and spoke quietly. "But let me make a couple of points before we begin."

"Okay, but if I'm going to call you Wendy, I'd prefer that you call me Joe." She nodded in response and then continued.

"As of the close of your fiscal year, exactly eight weeks ago today, Wilder Enterprises International generated 1.45 billion US dollars in worldwide revenues. Of that figure, more than six hundred fifty million was earned from the sale of items produced for or supplied to your company by Guangdong Light Industrial Products and its subsidiaries."

"How the hell did you get that information?" Joe Wilder was shocked. "We're not a public company!"

"You shouldn't underestimate China, Mr. Wilder." She smiled that same damn smile again. "We may be new to the finer points of capitalism, but we have been haggling in the marketplace for several thousand years."

"All right, you've made your point." Joe recovered quickly. "But if you just wanted to hold us up for a huge increase in prices, you didn't need to bring me all the way here. What do you really want?"

"That's true." She paused for a moment. "We are prepared to offer you a new ten-year irrevocable contract for all the items you presently buy from Guangdong Light Industrial as well as all of our subsidiaries. Prices will be fixed at last year's level, with no increases for the life of the contract."

"I would be crazy not to accept. Even if I don't increase my gross sales by one dollar, you're giving me a guaranteed net profit increase of twenty percent." Joe slowly shook his head. "You don't know me well enough to give me gifts like this. There's a big catch in here someplace. What do you want in return?"

"Of course, there are conditions to this kind of a proposal. In exchange for this favorable contract, you will agree to send at least one of your physical fitness training teams to China. Your team of experts will design and help to implement a physical fitness training program, using the Wilder methods, for our primary and secondary schools. We want the same Wilder fitness program that has been so successful in the American schools. You will also teach your training methods to one hundred of our instructors so that they can then teach others here in China." Wendy watched carefully as Joe made some quick calculations on a notepad. "If this is acceptable to you, I can have contracts ready tomorrow afternoon."

"If that's all there is to the conditions, then I think we have a deal." Joe stood and extended his hand to bind the agreement.

"Good!" Wendy rose, gripping his hand firmly and smiled warmly. The guarded shadow had disappeared. "Oh, there is one small personal favor that I would ask of you."

"What kind of personal favor?" Joe asked, suddenly wary.

"Something small, but we can discuss that tomorrow at my office in Beijing. Have you ever been to our capital?"

"No." Joe shook his head in surprise.

"Good, my office will make flight and hotel reservations for you." She smiled again, but this time her dark eyes sparkled with humor and a hint of mischief. "If we have time, I might even show you my ancestral home."

THREE

THE BEIJING OLYMPIC TOWER WAS ONE OF THOSE CONSTRUCTION projects rushed to completion before the opening ceremonies of the 2008 summer games. One square block of old, two-story, wood-frame structures had been demolished to make way for the thirty-two-story steel-and-black-glass-clad tower. Critics claimed that it resembled a giant rectangular Chinese black lacquer box that had been upended and hurriedly stuck in the ground. Others found the clean, black lines of the tower to be prime examples of modern architecture. The project was a joint venture between a small Chinese company, Beijing Development Partners, and a consortium of three European investment firms based in Switzerland.

Originally, the architect designed the project as a five-star luxury hotel with Western tourists and business travelers in mind. International brand-name boutiques filled the street-level mall, with a few high-end Chinese shops offering antiquities and porcelain works of art thrown into the mix. The first twenty-six floors were intended to be hotel rooms and suites, while the remaining floors were designed as elegant condominiums. Once under construction, Beijing Development Partners, as the managers of the project, changed the focus slightly to suit their own needs.

When it finally opened, the first thirty floors were luxury rooms and suites operated by the Hilton Hotel Corporation. Beijing Development Partners took the thirty first floor as its corporate headquarters and retained the penthouse, the entire thirty-second floor, as a private residence. The identity of the occupant was never disclosed, not even to the hotel staff. Access to the thirty second floor was limited to only one of the six elevators.

Whether by design or coincidence, one of the advantages of four separate entrances into the mall rotunda and hotel lobby was that it allowed four rather unremarkable Chinese gentlemen to make their way to the penthouse elevator unnoticed. The men were dressed similarly in dark business suits. Neither overly elegant nor flashy, they appeared to be simply well-dressed businessmen. Approaching the bank of elevators from different directions without acknowledging one another, they waited patiently for the small crowd to thin out before pressing the call button.

On the thirty-second floor, the elevator opened onto a large, windowless foyer paneled in lightly stained mahogany with a dark-granite tile floor. Two men sat behind a small security desk immediately to the right of a pair of eight-foot-tall, intricately carved, antique temple doors.

"Mr. Lin Zhang Lei, as always you are right on time." The lead security guard knew them all by sight, but he still went through the motions of comparing the man to the description in his logbook. Each man commanded a separate division of the Bai Lang army and reported to the Bai Lang personally at these monthly meetings. Sixty years old, he was the oldest of the inner circle. A heavyset man, strong as an ox, he had a nasty habit of cracking his knuckles. And he enjoyed hurting people. For the last thirty years, he had served as the chief enforcer for the Bai Lang army.

"Mr. Li Jun." The guard made a notation next to the name. Li Jun stood ramrod straight, the tallest of the group. His bearing and posture were the result of seven generations of army service and discipline. Convicted of corruption at the age of twenty, the Bai Lang had intervened in his court martial and saved him from prison. In return, Li Jun has devoted more than twenty years in service to his savior.

"Mr. Wang Ping, you missed the last meeting." The young guard knew that he overstepped his authority, but this man was the most amiable of the inner circle. He always seemed to have a kind word and ready smile. In his early forties, he was smaller than the others, with a thin, slight physique. Wang Ping had a reputation for being the toughest negotiator in the Far East.

"Mr. Sun Wang Ji, welcome. I believe this is your first meeting with the Bai Lang." At twenty-five years of age, he was the youngest member in the history of the organization to be named to the inner circle. The logbook described him as an avid sportsman with a penchant for blond European women, heavy metal music, and high-stakes poker. He seemed to be fidgety and ill at ease. The guard made a note of the apparent nervousness. He would report it to the Bai Lang after the meeting.

"Gentlemen, the Bai Lang is waiting." He stood and pressed a small button hidden on the underside of his desk, causing the massive temple doors to swing open silently.

"Please follow me." The young guard led them into the entry hall where a beautiful young Chinese woman wearing a knee-length, traditional, intricately embroidered Chinese silk dress and five-inch Italian stiletto heels bowed in greeting. The contrast of cultures was both beautiful and seductive. She followed the group down a wide hallway decorated with the same paneled walls and granite tile floor as the foyer. Six life-size terracotta warriors stood on either side of the hall, spaced some fifteen feet apart.

"Are these real?" Sun Wang Ji asked, reaching out to touch one of the figures.

"Please do not touch the warriors," the guard cautioned. "They are very old and delicate."

The penthouse was designed and furnished along Western lines, seemingly taken directly from the pages of *Architectural Digest*. With floor-to-ceiling windows, views of the city of Beijing stretched from the Forbidden City on the left to the striking modern buildings created for the Olympic Games to the south. Even from this height, the Drum and Water Towers appeared as twin monoliths, beacons to the older sections of the ancient city. On any clear night, the city lights were a carpet of bright colors that seemed to stretch to the horizon. The furniture was mostly of Italian design, modern lines with lots of steel, glass, and leather. The only Eastern element of the décor were the many antique Chinese porcelain, bronze, and ceramic figures displayed around the room.

Two life-size mannequins encased in glass stood on either side of the entrance to the room. One was dressed in an ancient suit of Chinese ceremonial armor inlaid with gold and silver, while the other figure wore the richly embroidered robes of an ancient emperor of China.

"Please be seated," the young woman said, then bowed, and followed the guard out of the room.

The four men took seats around the low coffee table and waited quietly. They never spoke among themselves before a meeting. The rules were clear: no alcohol, no smoking, and no notes.

"All right, let's get started," the Bai Lang said as he entered the room. He was a tall, handsome man in his late forties with just enough gray in his full head of hair to be the embodiment of the Bai Lang—*The White Wolf!* His custom-tailored Brioni suit did more to accentuate his athletic physique than hide it. As was his habit for these monthly meetings, he sat in a black leather Eames chair and faced the men.

Zhang Lei, the oldest man in the group, spoke up. "There is one problem that we need to talk about."

"Well?" The Bai Lang had other things on his agenda.

"Our contact in Vietnam, General Phan Lo, is demanding more money." He paused for a moment. "It seems that he has been monitoring our imports and calculated how much profit he thinks we're making while his people look the other way."

"What does he want?"

Sun Wang Ji picked up the narrative. "He wants us to double his fee, or else his people will start seizing our shipments and arresting our people."

"Impossible! Greed is such a terrible thing." The Bai Lang said quietly, then laughed. "Who is the next in line to take command if something happens to our friend General Phan Lo? Is it a relative?"

"No, he is a young and ambitious colonel."

"Tell the colonel that something tragic is about to happen to his boss and ask him if he would like to continue our relationship with a ten percent increase?"

"I am certain that he will be most honored to join our family." Zhang Lei smiled. "Timing is important because we have a very large shipment arriving in Ho Chi Min City in twelve days."

"Make him the offer today. If he accepts, make the general disappear in a very noisy, fiery way. Make it look like an accident, but make it obvious that we had a hand in his demise. And make sure that the word gets out that he tried to blackmail us."

"We can do it."

"No, I don't want anyone from our organization involved directly. Where is the German?"

"He is in Hong Kong," Wang Ping said softly.

"Good, have him take care of it." The Bai Lang changed the subject. "Now, what do we know about the woman?" He got to his feet and began pacing the room.

"We don't have any new information yet." As the youngest man in the group, Sun Wang Ji was assigned this task. "We have people searching through the birth records for three years before and after the date you gave us, but it will take some time. None of the records are computerized, so they all have to be examined by hand."

"Put more people on the search. We have to identify this woman quickly. There is nothing more important than finding her. She is the key to controlling half of China's economy. Call me when you have something."

The Bai Lang turned abruptly and left the room. The meeting had come to an end.

FOUR

THE ARCHED, VAULTED, AND COFFERED CEILING OF THE RAFFLES Beijing Hotel and the crystal chandeliers and Oriental rugs were lost on Joe at that moment. It was well after midnight, and he was exhausted. Joe checked in, took the envelope the clerk handed him, and followed the bellman to his suite. Between the delayed flight from Guangzhou and the jet lag, he desperately needed a good night's sleep.

Per the instructions in Wendy's note, Joe walked out of the hotel with his briefcase slung over his shoulder at eleven o'clock the next morning. She was already waiting for him, standing beside the open rear door of a Mercedes-Benz 500 S. She waited for him to slide in before walking around to the other side of the car.

"I thought that we could have an early lunch," Wendy said as their car worked its way through traffic. "There is a wonderful restaurant in Beihai Park called Fang Shan. I think that you will enjoy it."

"It's your city," Joe said with a smile. "I'm completely in your hands."

The ride through the city took less than twenty minutes even in the morning traffic. They skirted Tiananmen Square, circled the Forbidden City, and arrived at the east gate of the park. A short stroll along the river bordering the park brought them to a narrow stone bridge that crossed the river onto Jade Island.

As they approached the gated entrance to the restaurant, a pair of heavy wooden doors painted a bright shade of imperial red slowly swung open, allowing them to pass.

"Welcome to Fang Shan." Two hostesses dressed in elaborate Manchurian costumes ushered them into the first of the courtyards connecting the three very old, but impressive, Qing dynasty buildings. Each building was meticulously decorated in the imperial style with carved and painted beams. A number of red Chinese lanterns were strung from the eaves on either side of the courtyard.

"It's like stepping back into imperial China," Joe said as they were seated.

"The legend says this was the favorite restaurant of the Dowager Empress Cixi," Wendy said, smiling. "But I don't believe it."

"Oh, why not?"

"Because this place first opened in 1925, and Empress Cixi died in 1908." She laughed softly. "But it makes a great story for the tourists."

"Do you mind if I order for us?" Wendy pushed the menus aside. "On your first visit to Beijing, you should experience an emperor's meal!"

Somewhere between the bird's nest soup and the braised abalone and asparagus, Joe realized that he was enjoying her company and their light conversation. He didn't mind that she didn't seem to be in any hurry to finalize their business.

"So how did you choose the name Wendy?"

"I didn't. My sorority sister gave it to me." She laughed at his confused expression. "When I was accepted at UCLA, one of my professors told me not to be afraid to meet other students—don't stay just with the Chinese groups. He said you must get to know the Americans. So I rushed AEPi. They assigned me a big sister, Susie Steiner, to kind of take care of me. Susie couldn't pronounce Wen Shu Xian, so she started calling me Wendy, and that has been my Western name ever since."

"That took a lot of courage." Joe was impressed.

"I was very naïve." She laughed again. "I didn't know anything about sororities or how they worked. When I moved into the house, I discovered that most of the girls were Jewish. So I learned all about Passover, Chanukah, and the advantages of dating young Jewish men. It was great! We had two girls with long hair down to their waists. Susie Steiner, my big sister, was the brunette, and Susie Sterner was the blond. When boys would call and ask for Susie, we would ask, which one Sterner or Steiner? The boy usually didn't know the last name so they would say the one with long hair. Then we'd have to ask blond or brunette? Since my room was closest to the upstairs phone, I got most of the calls."

"How was it being the only Chinese woman in a Jewish sorority?" He asked, fascinated.

"It was wonderful! I got fixed up with dates for all the social events, and Susie introduced me to my first boyfriend." She paused, smiling at the memory. "His name was Jason. Actually, he was Susie's older brother. Jason took me to my first baseball game and introduced me to Dodger Dogs."

"He sounds like a terrible guy!" Joe smiled.

"I'm still a big Dodger fan and I love hot dogs," she admitted.

They had talked their way through several more courses and were just finishing the soft-fried prawns, duck-meat dumplings, and glazed fruit. Joe was pleased to discover that his "dragon lady" was delightfully charming, with a great sense of humor. He was beginning to develop a fondness for the woman.

"What happened to Jason?"

"We dated all through undergrad. Then he went to Columbia Law School, and I stayed at UCLA for my MBA." She said it almost wistfully.

"That must have been hard for you. It sounds like you had a very good relationship."

"It was hard at first, but when my cousin, Vicki, came to study English, it got better." She seemed to shake off the memory and glanced at her watch.

"Joe, the contracts won't be ready until after three this afternoon." The meal had finally come to an end. "And since it's not quite one o'clock, would you like to see my family home? It's very nearby."

"Sure, why not?" Joe thought it might help him to know her better, to understand her motivation.

Thanks in large part to the government license plates on the car, Wendy's driver was able to drop them in front of the Gate of Heavenly Peace, the first of three gates that guard the Forbidden City. She dismissed the driver, telling him they would walk back to her office at three o'clock. As she led Joe through the gate and gestured toward the Forbidden City.

"Welcome to the ancestral home of the Manchu emperors and the center of power in China for more than six hundred years." She smiled and waited a moment for his reaction.

"It's incredibly impressive." Joe turned a full 360 degrees to take in their surroundings and then followed her toward the Gate of Supreme Harmony.

Behind them, across Tiananmen Square, stood the imposing modern structures of the Great Hall of the People, the Museum of the Revolution, and the Tomb of Chairman Mao. Glancing first in one direction, then the other, Joe was struck by the contrasting images of ancient and modern China. Entering the Forbidden City, Joe felt as if they had stepped into a time warp. She led the way through the Meridian Gate, across the Inner Golden Water Bridge, and past the Gate of Supreme Harmony.

"I told you I was going to show you my family home," Wendy said as they crossed the square and began climbing the stairs leading to the Hall of Supreme Harmony.

"I'm sorry. I don't understand." His confusion deepened as Wendy stopped just inside the hall and pulled him off to the side of the entrance. As Joe's eyes adjusted to the change in light, he was treated to an incredible view of the ancient seat of power. A large beautiful, richly colored Chinese rug, depicting two dragons playing in the water, was spread before a large dais rising more than six feet above the floor. Three sets of carpeted stairs, each flanked by cloisonné tripods, led to the gilded throne in the center of the dais. The dais itself was roped off to prevent tourists from ascending to the golden throne.

Every inch of the double-beamed, coffered, and boxed ceiling, walls, and supporting pillars was richly painted, carved, and decorated with recurrent themes of dragons playing in water and amid the clouds. Six massive pillars, three on either side of the dais, measuring more than three and a half feet in diameter, towered some forty-two feet from floor to ceiling. Each pillar was painstakingly carved with serpentine dragon themes running its entire length. The gilding was both light- and dark-gold leaf to heighten the overall design in the ever-changing light of the room.

He noticed Wendy shifting her gaze quickly around the hall, carefully observing each group of tourists for a brief moment. It was early afternoon on a week day, so the clusters of visitors were relatively small, and they seemed to move on quickly. Wendy appeared to be searching for something. Finally, she was reassured that no one else was close enough to overhear them.

"You asked what I wanted in return for the new contracts. Well, now, in this place, at least for a few minutes, we can talk freely, and I can tell you." She waited for a moment as if gathering her courage. Wendy started to speak, then stopped, and sat down on the stone floor, leaning against a pillar facing the raised dais. Finally, her shoulders sagged a little, and she began quietly.

"That is the great Imperial Dragon Throne of the Manchu Qing emperors of China." She pointed to the center of the room and the intricately carved throne that sat on the elevated platform. "Only imperial dragons may have five claws. Did you know that? It is forbidden for anyone but the imperial family to use the five-claw image." For a moment, she sat silently enveloped in the grandeur of the Hall of Harmony.

"Only the Son of Heaven can sit on the Dragon Throne," she said simply.

"Who is the Son of Heaven?" Joe asked, sitting beside her.

"When a new emperor is crowned and sits on the throne for the first time, he is the Son of Heaven because he rules everything under heaven while the gods rule everything above." Wendy pointed to the sunken coffer in the center of the ceiling where two large, carved, and painted dragons seemed to be playing with a giant pearl. "Those silvery orbs are called the Xuan Yuan Mirror. They're made of glass and coated with mercury to reflect the light. The largest ball in the center, the pearl, is said to be able to tell a truth from a lie, to know good from evil, and it can even detect an imposter who sits on the throne trying to steal the power of China. If that happens, the great pearl will fall and kill the imposter."

"Remind me not to sit on the throne," Joe said, grinning.

"From the time of Qin Shi Huang, the dragon has been the symbol of the emperor."

"Who was he?"

"He was the first emperor of the Qin dynasty, the man who unified China. He created the Imperial Guard—a group of men known as the Dragon's Claw. If the symbol of the emperor is the dragon, the symbol of his power is the dragon's claw. The Imperial Guard was responsible for enforcing the wishes of the emperor and protecting the Imperial family. Each warrior was sworn to give his life to protect the Son of Heaven." She pointed to the largest dragon carved into the back rest of the throne. "Do you see the dragon with one leg thrust forward? Each member of the Imperial Guard received a dragon tattoo as a symbol of his enlistment. As a reward for their service, upon their death or retirement, a warrior was allowed to hand down his position in the guard to his son. From generation to generation, since the second century BC, the Dragon's Claw has always protected the emperor and the imperial family."

"That's an incredible story."

"Have you seen photographs of the Terracotta Army?"

"Sure," Joe said, nodding. "That's the silent army guarding the tomb of the first emperor, isn't it?"

"Each figure is unique and represents one of the original members of the Imperial Guard. They were the only people Qin Shi Huang trusted." Wendy got to her feet and began walking slowly toward the throne. When she reached the rope barring the steps leading up to the dais, she stopped.

"Did you ever see a movie called *The Last Emperor*?"

"Yes, but that was a long time ago," Joe replied, following her.

"In the movie, they said that the empress was pregnant during the Japanese occupation but the child died at birth." She stopped to look at him. "But the truth is that the empress was never pregnant."

"What are you trying to tell me?"

"Emperor Puyi, the last Manchu Qing dynasty emperor of China, married my mother in 1962." She seemed to be telling the story out loud for the first time. "They met here in Beijing. She was a nurse, and by then, he was an ordinary citizen of the People's Republic of China." Wendy moved around to the back of the throne platform, her fingers trailing across each pillar they passed.

"Are you telling me that you are the empress of China?" He was amused but then realized that she was serious.

"Yes." She ran her fingertips along the complex carving of one of the golden pillars. "But it's a secret, so don't tell."

It should have been a humorous statement, but her face was filled with sadness. Joe had the feeling that she was about to cry.

"My father was crowned emperor on this throne just before his third birthday. When I was a little girl, he would bring me here, and we would walk through the old palace buildings." Finally, a grin tugged at the corners of her mouth with the memory. "That was before the government turned it into a museum. He would tell me stories of his childhood and the secrets of the Forbidden City. Sometimes, when he was a little boy, he would try to get away from the eunuchs. He found dozens of places to hide. The eunuchs always searched for him, but they never found his secret places."

They were momentarily alone in the hall. Wendy reached up and quickly manipulated several pieces of the intricate carvings on the back of one pillar. After a moment, there was a muffled click, and a hidden drawer sprang open. Wendy reached in, retrieved a small package wrapped in brown paper and tied with twine, dropped it in her purse, and pushed the drawer closed. Afterward, on closer inspection, Joe couldn't find a trace of the opening. The sudden sounds of a group of school children crossing the terrace outside caught her attention.

"We must leave." Wendy led the way out the side entrance to the terrace and down the carved-stone steps. Once they were headed toward the Gate of Supreme Harmony and the Meridian Gate beyond, she slowed her pace. "We can talk privately for a while, as long as it isn't too crowded."

"Why are you telling me all of this?" Joe finally asked.

"I have a child." She stopped and faced him. "And that is why I need a small favor from you."

"How many people know your secret? Do people in the government know about you?"

"There are only a few—some very good friends. Some of my mother's friends are still alive, and of course, they know. A few of these are people of influence in the government."

"So, what exactly is this small favor you want from me?" They passed through the Tiananmen Gate, skirting the square, and continued walking slowly in the direction of the Ministry of Trade.

"My son is twelve years old," she said quietly. "He is the hereditary Manchu Qing dynasty emperor of China. He is the Son of Heaven. And I need your help to get him to America."

"Why on earth would you need my help?" Joe was at a loss. "You are the deputy minister of trade for the entire Guangdong province. I would think you have far more power than I have to get him out of the country."

"Three months ago, I was diagnosed with melanoma." She slowed her pace again as she spoke. "Since then, it has spread to my stomach. In spite of the chemotherapy, they tell me I only have a few months left."

"I am so sorry." Joe was genuinely moved. "But can't you use your contacts to get him a visa?"

"Getting a visa legally is not a problem, but there are powerful factions in China who suspect that my father left an heir. The Dragon's Claw still exists, and they still have some power in this country. Certainly, they will protect him, but I'm afraid that other groups, if they knew my son's true identity, would try to use him to restore the old empire along the lines of the British monarchy. Of course, any such attempt would be futile and bloody beyond imagination." She paused for a moment, allowing a small tour group to pass by. "More importantly, there is a third group, a tong known as the Bai Lang army. They are certain that I really exists and that I have a child. They desperately want to use him to expand their power."

"What do you mean?"

"They are part of a secret society dating back to the Opium Wars of the early 1800s. As a group, they are wealthy, powerful and very well connected within the People's Republic."

"Are they part of the government?"

"Not directly, but like your Mafia, they seem to have members or influence within the Central Committee. The Bai Lang believe my son is alive, but don't know who he is or where to find him. At least, not yet."

"What would happen if they found him?"

"Most certainly, he would be exploited or maybe killed."

"But I don't know what I can do to help? I can't smuggle him into the US, and I certainly can't break any laws here in China."

"You won't have to. I can legally arrange for the necessary travel documents, but he needs to have an American host, a sponsor, in order to leave China. He can travel as an exchange student, just like I did. Are you willing to help me?" They had reached the entrance to the Ministry of Trade. "I will sign the new contracts either way."

"Do you have any idea how fantastic this all sounds?" They stood silently for a moment. Joe studied her face intently before answering, all the while memories of that day in Paris came screaming back into his consciousness. The sights, sounds, and smell of the fight—the weight of a boy's lifeless body in his arms.

"All right, Wendy, I'll do everything I can to help him get to America." He reached out to shake her hand and bind their agreement. "I promise you: no harm will come to your son."

"Thank you." She gripped his hand tightly as her eyes filled with tears. "It will take a day or two for the papers, but I will have someone contact you at your hotel tomorrow." Her expression reflected the relief she felt.

"There's just one more thing." Wendy reached into her purse for the small package and handed it to Joe."

"What is this?"

"This is the Imperial Seal of the first emperor of China. It's more than two thousand years old, and it's my son's heritage. I know you are a man of influence. When you get home, would you please give this to your Secretary of State?"

"Okay." Joe turned the small bundle over in his hands, wondering what he'd gotten himself into before slipping it into his briefcase. "Is there anything else I should know?"

"No, that's everything." She smiled again, as if a great burden had been lifted from her shoulders. "Now, I think we have some contracts to sign."

THE ADDENDUMS AND REVISIONS KEPT THEM WORKING THROUGH the dinner hour. By the time the final versions were signed and recorded with the Ministry of Trade, it was past seven o'clock in the evening. Finally, it was done, and they were alone in the conference room.

"Thank you again, Joe." Wendy extended her hand, her gratitude evident in her face. "It has been a pleasure getting to know you."

"The pleasure has been mine." Instead of taking her hand, Joe reached his arms around her in a gentle hug. "Are you sure you won't come to Los Angeles for a second opinion? You know, UCLA still has a pretty good medical center."

"I'm sure, but thank you." She took his hand in hers and held it for a long moment.

"Does your son know?"

"Yes, he does." There was a moment of sadness, but then she brightened. "Have a good evening. My driver will take you back to the hotel."

After FedExing the contracts to Millie, Joe stepped into the empty elevator, pressed the button for the top floor and then leaned against the wall. He was bone tired and still operating on Los Angeles time.

Maybe room service and a hot shower, he thought, *or maybe just the hot shower.*

Once in the suite, he locked and chained the door before dropping his briefcase on the bed and heading to the bathroom to wash his hands.

The miniature scanner was in his shaving kit exactly where he'd left it. It didn't really matter how tired he was, Joe always checked the room. It was an old habit, a quirk left over from that previous life, but one he could not overlook. And, as before, the scanner found the suite was free of any surveillance.

After a hot shower, Joe wrapped himself in the plush bathrobe the hotel had so thoughtfully provided, and went to the small bar in the living room. He filled a glass with ice and vodka and then found a comfortable spot on the sofa. Wendy's package was sitting on the coffee table in front of him.

What the hell am I going to do with you? he thought.

Looking around the room, there didn't seem to be an obvious place to hide it. Of course, there was the safe in the bedroom closet, but a blind dog with a strong tail could open it. He chuckled at the mental image.

"I am too tired for this now," he muttered.

Finally, he found a safe place to put the package. It only took a few minutes work with his Swiss Army knife to remove the vent cover above the entry hall. He wrapped the package in a plastic hotel laundry bag, placed it inside the air conditioning duct, and replaced the vent cover.

When he was finished, Joe examined his handiwork. It wasn't perfect, but it would do for the moment. The housekeeping staff was very thorough and kept the room free of dust. As a result, there were no telltale smudges on the vent cover to indicate it had been touched. Satisfied, he went to bed.

FIVE

By nine o'clock the next morning, Joe's life had returned to its normal level of mild chaos. After a one hour workout in the hotel gym, a quick shower, and change of clothes, Joe was working his way through breakfast while simultaneously holding a Skype conference on his laptop computer and a conference call on his cell phone. It was only six in the evening in Los Angeles, and his obligations under the new contract required a lot of scheduling. In the midst of all this turmoil, two housekeepers were busily trying to put the suite in order.

"Can we come in?" Three men stood at the open door to the suite. "We are sorry to disturb you, Mr. Wilder, but it is very important."

"Sure." Joe waved them toward seats on the couch before turning his attention back to the laptop and his cell phone. "Phil, can you work with Millie to arrange the schedules? Your contact here is a Mr. Tony Wang in Wendy's office. I want to get the training teams in place as soon as possible. There are some people here now, so I'm going to sign off." He turned off the cell phone and shut down the computer before turning his attention to the three strangers.

"My name is Michael Fitzpatrick, Mr. Wilder." The tall blond American got to his feet and extended a hand to Joe. "I'm the senior trade attaché at the US embassy here in Beijing." Joe sensed something unsettling in his tone of voice.

"This is Police Inspector Chou Kong-Sang and his partner, Detective Yuen Woo." Joe shook hands with the somber-faced inspector. He was a good-looking man with short-cropped, salt-and-pepper hair, a little shorter than his companion, with a thin build. On the other hand, his partner was a giant—over six feet tall and weighing well over two hundred pounds.

"I don't understand. What do you want with me?" Joe asked.

Before he responded, Inspector Chou waved the two housekeepers out of the suite, waiting until the door was closed behind them.

"Do you know Miss Wen Shu Xian?" Inspector Chou asked. He spoke excellent, heavily accented English.

"You must already know that I do. Otherwise, you wouldn't be here. What's going on, Inspector?" Joe took a seat opposite the police officer.

"When was the last time you saw her?" The Inspector ignored his question.

"We spent most of yesterday together. It was probably seven o'clock in the evening by the time we finished our business. I left her office and came straight back here."

"Did you hear from her or anyone from her office after that time?"

"No." Joe frowned. He was getting irritated with the inspector's tone. "Would you mind telling me what the hell is going on?"

"I'm sorry to tell you that Wen Shu Xian died last night."

No matter how someone tried to soften the news, Joe knew it was the kind of bombshell police inspectors hated to deliver.

"Oh my God, what happened?" Joe slumped back into his chair, the shock evident in his expression. "I knew that she had health problems, but I didn't think she was that bad."

"What do you mean?" It was the detective's turn to be surprised.

"Wendy told me that she had cancer and that her treatment wasn't going well."

"Huh." Inspector Chou sat quietly for a few moments, obviously mulling over this new information. "I must tell you that her illness was not the cause of her death. Wen Shu Xian may have fallen, jumped, or been pushed out of her eighth-floor office window. We are not certain."

"I don't believe it!" Joe remembered Wendy's description of the Bai Lang and their desperation to find her.

"Why on earth would anyone want to hurt her?" Joe looked from the inspector to the trade attaché.

"Like your Mafia they seem to have members or influence in the Central Committee." Wendy's words of caution were fresh in his memory. Could the police inspector be trusted?

"I was hopeful you could tell us." Inspector Chou was watching Joe's reactions carefully. Detective Yuen Woo finally spoke up, saying something to Chou in Chinese. The inspector nodded and then continued. "The office was very messed up, drawers pulled out and files thrown everywhere. They were searching for something they did not find."

"How do you know they didn't find what they were looking for?"

"We know." Chou shrugged. "It is my opinion that Wen Shu Xian jumped out of the window so that she would not have to give them what they wanted."

"What the hell is going on here?" Joe asked.

Fitzpatrick finally spoke up. "You spent the entire day with Wendy yesterday. Did she seem nervous or worried about anything?"

"You mean besides her cancer?" Joe shook his head slowly. "No, there was nothing at all."

They spent another thirty minutes going over the details of their day together. Finally, the inspector seemed to run out of questions to ask.

"If you remember anything that might help us, please call me." Inspector Chou got to his feet and handed Joe his business card. He stopped at the door with one more comment. "I hope that you are planning to stay in Beijing for a few more days, Mr. Wilder. It really is a beautiful city." The two policemen closed the door behind them, leaving Fitzpatrick behind.

"Anything you want to tell your embassy representative now that we are alone?"

"No." Joe crossed the room to the bar and filled a glass with ice and vodka. "Do you want something?"

"No, thanks, it's still a little early for me."

"Yeah, but its six o'clock last night in LA." He swirled the liquid in his glass sadly. "Am I really a suspect?"

"No. It's just the way they do things here." Fitzpatrick glanced at his watch. "What are you going to do today?"

"I have no idea." He drained his drink. "Any suggestions?"

"Sure," Fitzpatrick said. "Do some sightseeing. This is a great city. You'll spend a day or two here and then head for home." He handed Joe a business card. "I'll send a car to pick you up at seven tomorrow evening. Knowing how friendly you are with the president, when the ambassador heard you were in town, he insisted on inviting you to the reception he's hosting for some congressmen. The chairman of the House Appropriations Committee is the guest of honor. He's a friend of yours too, isn't he?" He didn't wait for a reply. "If you need anything, my cell phone number is on the card."

"Thanks," Joe said and shook the diplomat's hand before he left, then locked the door.

When he was finally alone, Joe stood on a chair and used his Swiss Army knife to remove the air conditioner vent cover from the soffit over the entry hall. Looking into the duct, Joe couldn't see the package at first. Reaching back into the duct around the first bend of sheet metal, he stretched until his fingers found Wendy's package.

Placing the parcel on the coffee table, Joe stared at it for several minutes. Carefully, he untied the twine and removed the old brown paper, revealing an exquisite black lacquered box. It was decorated with the image of an imperial dragon made of green-and-white jade inlaid into the lid. He guessed the box measured some six by eight inches with a depth of no more than four inches. A gold clasp held the lid closed.

When Joe opened the box, he found the inside divided into two silk-lined compartments. The smaller of the two sections held a piece of jade five inches tall with a two-inch square base. He recognized the imperial dragon image etched into two of the four sides of the stone. The remaining sides were etched with Chinese letters or characters. As Joe turned the jade in his hands, he noticed the carving on the underside. One corner of the figure seemed to have been broken off and replaced with gold.

"So, this is the Heirloom Seal of the Realm," Joe whispered, almost reverently. Gently, he replaced the jade in the special section of the box and cautiously removed the folded parchment from the other compartment. Although he had no idea how long it had been hidden in the gold pillar of the Hall of Harmony, the document appeared to be quite old and in remarkably good condition. Carefully, he unfolded the paper and spread it across the table.

The single sheet of elaborate text was a little difficult to decipher at first. After a second run through, the importance of the document became abundantly clear.

Whereas the Eight Nation Alliance hereby acknowledges the unparalleled assistance of the Dowager Empress Cixi in bringing about a peaceful resolution to the attacks on foreign citizens within the Empire of China, we do hereby mutually agree to modify a portion of the Boxer Protocol: To wit, the United States of America shall return to China that certain portion of the indemnification in the amount of $11,961,121.61 for the express purpose of constructing the Tsinghua University in Beijing. Moreover, the United States of America shall hold an additional amount of money in trust for the benefit of his Imperial Highness, the Emperor of China, his heirs and the Imperial family to be termed the EEF and paid upon demand as directed by the beneficiaries. Lastly, in the event of revolution, insurrection or abdication, the United States of America will give asylum to and guarantee the safety of his Imperial Highness, the Emperor of China, his descendants, heirs and the Imperial family without reservation or limit.

Signed this 7 day of February, 1908,

Theodore Roosevelt
President of the United States

Elihu Root
Secretary of State

Stunned, Joe sat staring at the single sheet of paper for several minutes before folding it gingerly and replacing it in the lacquered box. Once it was rewrapped in the brown paper, Joe secured the twine and placed a small length of red thread from the hotel sewing kit in the center of the bow. Unless you were looking for it, the one-inch-long thread would go unnoticed, but if the twine were removed or untied, the thread would fall away—a sure sign the package had been tampered with. Afterward, he placed it back in the air conditioning duct. His only option was to wait for the contact Wendy had promised would come today or tomorrow. The smart move, Joe decided, was to resume the appearance of normalcy or as close to it as he could get under the circumstances. Basically, he went back to work.

THE INTRICACIES OF SENDING A TRAINING TEAM OF TWELVE PEOPLE to Beijing for six to eight months required a great deal of logistical coordination. Thank God for Millie and her organizational skills.

Calling Millie back, Joe restarted the conversation the visit from Inspector Chou had interrupted.

"Phil, we should probably wait a few days before you contact Tony Wang," Joe suggested. "I'm sure that office is going to be messed up for a while."

"It will take me at least a week to pull the team together," Phil responded. "In the meantime, Millie, do you need anything else from me?"

"No, but if I do, I know where to find you." Millie waited until Phil disconnected from their conference call. "Joe, are you okay?"

"Thanks, Millie, I'm all right." He checked his watch. It was very late in Los Angeles. "Go on home. I'll call you tomorrow."

By the time he had finished some paperwork and sent a few emails, it was one o'clock in the afternoon, and he had run out of things to do. He had avoided thinking about Wendy and her son. There was very little he could do at this point but wait to hear from Wendy's contact. There was no reason to sit in the hotel room any longer.

Fitzpatrick said I should do some sightseeing, Joe thought.

six

FOLLOWING THE MAP KURT THE CONCIERGE HAD PROVIDED, JOE
came out of the hotel, walked down the sloping driveway, and turned right
onto Changan Avenue. The sidewalks that bordered this famous boulevard
were wide and filled with people. It seemed to be an equal mix of Chinese
and Europeans, tourists, and businessmen and -women.

He set a leisurely pace, moving along the crowded street toward
Tiananmen Square. Joe turned left on Guangchang East Side Road,
walking past the National Museum of China, and paused in front of the
Ministry of Trade. Two uniformed policemen stood by the barricades that
partially blocked the entrance. Looking up, Joe saw workers repairing
a window on the eighth floor. After a moment, he turned and walked
diagonally across the square.

Following Kurt's yellow-highlighted line on the map, he walked for
another ten minutes before reaching the start of the Dashilan Commercial
Street. According to the historical notes on his map, the street has been

a bustling shopping attraction for more than 580 years where crowds of tourists from all over the world, including China, vied for bargains large and small. Most of the architecture seemed to be either ancient and well preserved or faithful reproductions of the Ming and Qing dynasties. As promised, there were crowds of tourists working their way along the street, stopping at the various shops, some buying, others merely window shopping. Genuine antiques shared shelf space with extremely good copies and waited for the connoisseur, or the sucker, with a credit card. He passed shop windows displaying everything from designer women's handbags and Italian shoes to jewelry, toys, medicinal herbs, and teas.

Joe meandered along the lane, periodically entering one shop or another, looking but not really shopping for souvenirs. He was fascinated by the negotiating antics of both buyers and sellers that he observed along the way. After stepping into the Rui Fu Xiang silk shop, where his senses were assaulted by a limitless selection of colors and designs. Imperial red and yellow seemed to be the dominant shades in the bolts of material on display. As he made his way out of the shop, Joe finally began to think about Wendy.

One thing seemed certain, he thought, *if she jumped from the window, it was to protect her son. If that's the case, the secret of her son's identity died with her.*

Undoubtedly, whoever confronted Wendy in her office would now be searching for the boy. With the mother dead, they would assume the boy did not have the support he needed to remain hidden. Joe didn't like giving the opposition the first move; it made him feel powerless.

This is pointless! I have to wait.

He wandered into the Ma Ju Yuan hat shop and was promptly greeted by a sales woman. She informed him that their shop has been making hats for government officials, visiting dignitaries and various Chinese minorities for more than 185 years. Although he was impressed, Joe tried to explain that he didn't wear hats very often. He exited the shop as gracefully as possible and continued down Dashilar Street.

The guide map said that Nei Lian Sheng had the finest handmade shoes for men, women, and children in all of China. Joe looked in the window but continued down the road. His sole purpose in coming to the Dashilar district was to find a simple, small gift for Millie. So far, he hadn't seen anything that would fit the bill.

As he neared the end of the lane, Joe noticed that some of the shops were closing up for the day. It was nearly six o'clock when he saw a beautiful Tang dynasty glazed horse in a shop window. The signs said they sold only the finest quality old and new genuine antiques. Joe entered the shop with a smile.

"How much for the small Tang dynasty horse in the window?" he asked.

"You have very good eye!" the proprietor exclaimed. "This horse is very beautiful."

"How much?"

"Not enough—seven hundred fifty dollahs." He was a little old man with a wrinkled, weather worn face, bright eyes and a friendly smile.

"Too much!" Joe said.

"How much you pay?" He brought the horse out of the window and set it on the shop counter.

"I don't want to hurt your feelings. You give me your best price."

"I give you my best horse!" He fiddled with an abacus for a moment. "You give me five hundred dollah."

"You are a very good businessman, but I can't pay so much for this small horse." Joe examined the figure, turning it over and around in his hands. It stood about fifteen inches tall and eighteen inches wide. "I'll give you two hundred dollars."

"No!" The old man yelled something in Chinese, and a moment later a young boy came in from the back room. The two spoke for a few minutes, and then the old man smiled at Joe.

"Best price four hundred dollah."

"My best price is three hundred dollars." Joe was enjoying the game.

"Okay, okay." The old man handed the horse to the boy who wrapped it in paper and placed it in a large plastic bag with two handles. "You make good deal."

"Now, is this a real Tang horse?" Joe asked, handing the proprietor the cash.

"No, is ceramic Tang horse," the shopkeeper retorted. "If it real horse, you must clean up shop!" He laughed at his own joke. "You pay fair price for good copy. You want give me back?"

"No. You're right. It is a fair price." Joe grinned again and shook the old shopkeeper's hand. "Can you tell me where I can find a taxicab?"

"Where you want to go?"

"Do you know the Skewered Tobacco Pouch Street?" Joe pulled out his map and laid it on the counter.

"Oh, good place! You like won tons and roast pork?" He pointed to three restaurants marked on the map. "This Master Hou, he has best won tons in Beijing. Here is Master Yao, very good roast pork. This one is Master Ji, but I no like lamb."

The taxi dropped him off at the east end of a narrow lane that was a little more than 250 yards long. Once known as the only place in Beijing to buy tobacco and pipes, it had become a tourist site with shops selling Chinese and Tibetan costumes, pottery, badges, quotations of Chairman Mao, and various souvenirs. Interspersed with these shops are a wide range of restaurants offering specialized dishes from all over Asia.

Master Hou was more or less toward the middle of the block. It was a small and well-laid-out restaurant with white tablecloths and napkins that seemed to invite tourists. This was dining rather than just eating a quick meal on the run. Most of the tables were occupied, but Joe was able to choose one to the right of the entrance and against the wall. He was only slightly amused by the realization that his choice of this particular table put his back to the wall but gave him a clear line of sight to the large front window as well as both doors. *Old habits and good training*, he thought with a smile.

"Would you like a Tsing Tao?" a waiter asked as he placed an English language menu on the table.

"Sure." Joe replied, leaning his chair back against the wall. A few minutes later, the waiter returned with the beer and Master Hou.

"I am honored to have you in my humble restaurant, Mr. Wilder." The chef spoke excellent English. "My son is a great fan. Your pictures are everywhere in his room. He wants to be a great body builder like you."

"Thank you." Joe smiled, a little embarrassed.

"No menu, I will choose for you." The chef was beaming. "You will enjoy my food. I promise."

Joe took his time working through five courses of won ton and two bottles of beer. While he enjoyed the meal, he allowed his mind to wander back to the problem at hand. Wendy had said that someone would contact him, but when? Was she able to contact that person before she was confronted in her office? More importantly, was the boy safe and if so, for how long?

He asked for the check and signed an autograph for Master Hou's son. It was eight o'clock by the time Joe stepped out of the restaurant, turning to the left in the direction of a taxi stand. The street was narrow and fairly dark as it curved slightly to the right. At that hour of the evening, the shops and most of the restaurants were closed. The crowds had thinned out, leaving only the occasional pedestrian and giving the ancient street a deserted feeling. Joe quickened his pace, trying to walk off a little of the won ton dinner and beer. Coming around the small bend in the road, he noticed two men walking side by side toward him. There was nothing remarkable about them, yet they drew his attention immediately. Joe slowed his pace, trying to find whatever it was that made him uneasy.

Suddenly, he realized the men were moving in unison, shoulder to shoulder, each swinging their outside arm in a normal way as they walked. The odd thing was that their inside arms were fixed at their sides, not in a pocket, but hidden behind the seam of a pant leg. It was so unnatural that it had jarred Joe's subconscious. What were they hiding?

Joe shifted the bag containing his Tang dynasty horse to his left hand as he changed direction slightly to the center of the lane. Closing the gap between them, he tried to appear as nonchalant as possible while concentrating on the two hidden hands. Then, in a brief flash, he saw it. The man on the left held a syringe, but the other man's hand was still hidden from view. The two men separated, moving to the sides of the street ostensibly allowing Joe to pass between them. It was a simple, classic trap.

They were no more than ten feet away when Joe suddenly rushed forward, closing the gap. The two men were taken completely off guard as Joe swung the ceramic horse in a vicious backhand arch, bringing it crashing into the first assailant's face, crushing his nose and breaking several teeth. The syringe dropped to the ground as the man, and shattered ceramic horse, toppled backward, crashing through a shop window.

The second man, shocked for a split second, lunged forward, the knife in his hand suddenly all too visible. Joe sidestepped the thrust and smashed his fist into the assailant's cheek, shattering the zygomatic arch, sinuses, and jaw with one powerful blow. The man lay motionless in the street. Joe kicked the knife away before turning his attention back to the first man.

"Who are you?" Joe demanded as he pulled the first man out of the broken shards of glass that had once been a shop window. The man managed to mumble something unintelligible before slipping into unconsciousness. Joe laid him on the ground and began searching his pockets.

"What you do? What happen my shop?" The nearly hysterical shopkeeper, yelling in Chinese and English, had come out of the back room at the sound of his window being destroyed.

"Call the police," Joe said calmly and firmly as he continued to search his assailant's pockets.

The police had arrived very quickly after the attack and were quite thorough in their investigation. The two men were taken to the hospital under guard and would be questioned as soon as they regained consciousness.

"We have to stop meeting like this." Joe told Inspector Chou without humor. He had given the detective a clear and accurate report of the incident from the moment he left the restaurant.

"Do you have any idea why they attacked you?" The Inspector leaned against the police car next to Joe.

"I don't have a clue."

"Well, they had no identification of any kind." He pulled a notepad from his coat pocket and began flipping through several pages. "It was a good thing you spotted that syringe. It was loaded with enough ketamine to put a water buffalo to sleep."

"How do you know what was in the syringe?" Joe asked.

"The glass vial you found on the guy with the broken jaw was half filled with it."

"I don't understand. If they wanted to kill me, why not just shoot me?"

"I think they wanted to take you prisoner, not kill you," Inspector Chou replied, thoughtfully. "The medical team told me that ketamine would have turned you into a puppet. You would not have had the will to resist."

"Why? What do they want?"

"I hope, when the two men in the hospital wake up, they will tell us."

"Do you think this has anything to do with Wendy?" Joe already knew the answer.

"We will see ... probably." He regarded Joe carefully. "Is there something you want to tell me?"

"So, what happens now, Inspector?" Joe ignored the question.

"We have statements from you and the other witnesses." The detective stood up and stretched his back. Obviously, he had put in a long day. "For now, I will have a car take you back to your hotel, and you can go back to your life." He stood there for a long moment. "May I ask, how did you know?"

"It was just ..." Joe shrugged. "When I saw them coming toward me, there was just something off."

"You should be very careful now, I think."

SEVEN

THE NEXT MORNING WAS A REPEAT OF THE PREVIOUS DAY. A QUICK workout, a shower, and change of clothes was followed by Skype conference calls with the WEI offices in Los Angeles. There was a certain comfort in the normalcy of the routine. However, Joe carefully avoided mentioning the events of the previous evening. There was no reason to alarm Millie at this point.

By ten o'clock, most of Joe's business day was complete. He wondered if it could be this easy once he was back home. It was an appealing thought, interrupted by a knock on the door.

"Housekeeping!" a disembodied voice said through the door.

"Come in!" Joe shouted just as the hotel house phone began ringing.

"Do you think you can stay out of trouble long enough to come to our party tonight?" It was evident that Michael Fitzpatrick was a devoted fan of his own humor.

"I'll do my best." Joe had recognized the voice immediately. "Have you heard anything new?"

"No, the police haven't been able to question your two friends yet. The guy you hit is still in surgery."

"That's too bad," Joe said.

"What the hell did you hit him with, a sledgehammer? I saw the X-rays. That guy is a mess."

"I just used my fist," Joe replied. "But you have to remember that I've been working out with two-hundred-pound dumbbells since I was fifteen."

"Yeah, well, that'll teach these guys not to pick on Americans in the future," Fitzpatrick said. Joe sensed that the trade delegate was enjoying the situation in a very perverse way. "And speaking of picking on Americans, Inspector Chou and I both got phone calls from the deputy minister of justice this morning."

"Why would he call you?" Joe asked.

"He said he was concerned about a prominent American businessman being attacked in Beijing. He's just a nice guy worried about their public image." Fitzpatrick's sarcasm wasn't lost on Joe.

"Sure, he is."

"Okay, don't forget: the embassy car will pick you up at seven this evening. Wear a suit so you look like you belong." The fact that Joe was a frequent visitor to the White House and a major power broker in California politics was well known. But Fitzpatrick seemed to enjoy the banter.

"Okay, okay, I'll be ready." Joe put down the phone.

"Excuse me, Mr. Wilder." He hadn't realized the housekeeper had been standing behind him for some time.

"Yes?"

"If you are not busy today, I think you would like to visit Chao Yang Park?" The young woman smiled. "There you will see the Beijing International Kite Festival."

"And why would I want to do that?" he asked, studying her carefully, looking for any sign of a threat.

"You will see many things in the park. Especially near the fountain at the north end. There are benches nearby, and it is a good place to eat lunch." She smiled again.

"What kind of things do you think I will see?" He suddenly realized that she was not a hotel maid.

"You should go around noon time, I think. Take a lunch to the benches on the north end." She turned to leave the room and then stopped. "You can watch the Kite Festival preparations, and you might even see the Son of Heaven."

Joe sat quietly for a few minutes after she had gone, contemplating the enigmatic message he had just received. Wendy had said he would be contacted, but she hadn't indicated how or by whom. Obviously, these were the people taking care of the boy, but what about the opposition? Should he contact the police? What about Fitzpatrick? No, that would be pointless. What could a trade attaché do in this kind of situation? How the hell did he get himself into this mess?

Who are you kidding? he thought. *You're enjoying the intrigue and the danger! You haven't had an adrenaline rush like this in years.*

Joe checked the time and then began putting together the items he would need for this outing. Snatching the small backpack provided by the hotel, he quickly filled it with two small bottles of water, some fresh fruit from the bowl on the coffee table, two bags of nuts from the minibar and his Swiss Army knife. Almost as an afterthought, he grabbed sunglasses, a baseball cap, his Nikon, and a lightweight jacket out of his carry-on and hurried out the door.

Donning the blue cap and matching jacket as he exited the hotel, he assumed they would make him easier to follow. Ignoring the taxi line, he turned right along Changan Avenue and began walking toward the

Forbidden City at a fairly leisurely pace. Turning down the first side street and walking on for another half block, he stopped several times to look in shop windows. In reality, he was using the windows to see if he was being followed. The tail was easy to spot. Joe recognized them as the detectives who had driven him back to the hotel. Sitting in their car, they watched from a comfortable distance somewhat less than fifty yards away. Obviously, Inspector Chou's orders were to observe but not interfere.

After making a show of checking his street map, Joe crossed the little side street and headed back to Changan Avenue passing the plainclothes police officers. Turning toward the Forbidden City again, Joe quickened his stride. It wouldn't do to have them too close for the next few minutes.

On the edge of Tiananmen Square, he joined a large group of tourists as they jostled one another to board their tour bus. Joe moved to the inner edge of the crowd between the tourists and the bus. Dropping down on one knee, he was momentarily hidden from the observers view. Quickly removing the baseball cap and jacket, he shoved them into the backpack, stood up, and joined the crowd again. As he neared the front of the bus, Joe moved around to the far side of the vehicle. A taxi had just dropped off a fare. He jumped in the back seat and quickly gave the driver directions to the east gate of Chao Yang Park.

Measuring nearly two miles long and one mile wide, Chao Yang is the largest park in Beijing. Consisting of two public swimming pools, a roller coaster, a Ferris wheel, two lakes, gardens, walking trails, a concert stage, and huge, open grassy fields, it was designed to rival the great city parks of the Western world.

Entering the park through the eastern gate, Joe retrieved the baseball cap as he carefully worked his way around the roller coaster and beach-volleyball stadium, heading more or less in the direction of the kite-festival practice area. He walked casually, stopping once in a while to take some pictures. A typical tourist enjoying the largest park in Beijing. The sunglasses and cap effectively hid his face from any curious onlookers.

It was a little before noon when Joe reached the fountain. He picked a stone bench just to the right of the fountain that was shaded by some trees. From this vantage point, he had a sweeping view of the large grass field where some one hundred kites were being launched, flown, recovered, and repaired in preparation for the opening ceremonies. According to the guide map, more than one thousand kites from all over the world would be flown on Saturday to begin the week-long Beijing International Kite Festival. Some kites were single-pilot affairs, while others required teams of six or eight operators to keep them airborne. A group of ten school children were valiantly trying to launch a dragon kite, while proud parents and teachers watched from the sidelines.

Joe took some pictures of the more dramatic and colorful kites before setting aside his camera. Spreading his lunch out on the bench beside him, he made a show of leisurely enjoyment. After ten or fifteen minutes, a young woman from the group of parents approached him carrying her own lunch.

"May I share your bench?" she asked.

"Sure." Joe moved down to give her more room. He guessed her age to be early forties. She was tall, with a slim, athletic figure and a beautiful face enhanced by high cheekbones and full lips heightened with only a hint of makeup. Her long, dark hair was pulled back into a ponytail beneath a baseball cap of her own.

"Your photos don't do you justice, Mr. Wilder." She spoke softly, never looking directly at him. "Wendy has told me much about you."

"I'm sorry to say that she has told me nothing about you," he responded.

"My name is Vicki Mou. Wendy was my cousin." Finally, she faced him. "Didn't she say I would contact you?"

"Not you specifically, just that someone would be in touch with me."

They ate in silence for a few minutes. A casual observer would simply assume they were two people sharing a bench and nothing more.

"I am very sorry about Wendy," Joe said, finally.

"Thank you." She seemed to be watching the children struggle with the kite.

"You speak English very well," he observed.

"I was an English major at UCLA with Wendy. Now, I teach English to these children." They sat in silence for several minutes before she continued. "Will you meet me tomorrow morning at the top of the Drum Tower?"

"Why? Can't we talk here?"

"No, not really, and we need to make some plans very quickly." Now, she turned slightly, looking directly at him. "I would not like them to attack you again."

"What time?"

"Ten o'clock." Vicki smiled and then turned her attention to the school children. The dragon kite soared upward for a brief moment and then suddenly plunged to the ground. As the children surrounded the downed kite, Vicki yelled something in Chinese and waved one of the boys to come over.

"Chao Li, this is Mr. Wilder." Standing before Joe was a handsome boy, eleven or twelve years of age, slightly more than five feet tall with thick, longish black hair.

"It is nice to meet you, sir." They shook hands formally. "My American name is Charley." Despite an infectious grin, there was a sadness showing in his eyes.

"It's nice to meet you too, Charley."

"You better go back to the group," Vicki said. The boy waved and ran off.

"He's a good-looking boy." Joe watched him help stretch the dragon kite out on the grass to its full length.

"He's very bright and a very good student. And if we can't get him out of the country soon, I'm afraid they are going kidnap him or kill him." She said it quietly, sadly, in a matter-of-fact tone.

"I'll see you tomorrow." Joe packed up his gear and headed back the way he had come without looking back at her or the boy.

THE NEW MASSIVE AMERICAN EMBASSY COMPOUND BORE A STRONG resemblance to a high-rise office building and shopping-center complex that had miraculously been dropped into the middle of the Chinese capital. It is an elegant array of modern structures built of glass, steel, and marble that stood in sharp contrast to the surrounding classical architecture of old China.

Embassy parties around the world have an undeniable sameness to them. A security staffed entrance—metal detectors and all—followed by the traditional receiving line. Joe worked his way down the line, greeting the ambassador and his wife before moving on to the guest of honor, Congressman Adam Schreiber, longtime chairman of the House Appropriations Committee.

"It's good to see you, Joe." They shook hands warmly. "I'm surprised to find you in Beijing. I hope we'll have a chance to talk privately later this evening."

"I hope so, Congressman. If not, let's make some plans once we get back to LA."

Joe threaded his way through the crowd into the reception hall. As he stood in a line six deep at the bar, he was wondering why he'd bothered to come tonight.

"You don't want any of that stuff." Michael Fitzpatrick, a glass in each hand, nudged Joe's shoulder. "Come with me. I got this special liquid fire from the Russian trade attaché last week." He handed Joe a glass of vodka over ice and led the way to a group of chairs at the far end of the room.

"That was a cute trick you pulled today with the tour bus. Someone might think you were still an active field agent." Fitzpatrick smiled. "Inspector Chou was fit to be tied."

"I'm just an old, overweight businessman," Joe said.

"Tell that to the two guys you put in the hospital!" Fitzpatrick laughed.

"I just needed some time alone." Joe smiled in return and raised his glass in salute. "To your health, sir."

"Same to you." Fitzpatrick paused for a minute, sipping his drink. A waiter brought a bowl of ice cubes and the bottle of Russian vodka, placing them on the table between the two men. When the waiter had moved out of earshot, he continued. "So, what did you think of Vicki?"

"I take it you're not just a trade attaché?"

"Let's just say we're shorthanded, and I try to do whatever I can to fill in." He smiled briefly and leaned forward before continuing. "I helped Wendy as much as I could, but there are limits to what I can do inside China."

"I assume you took care of the visa."

"Yes, it was the least I could do. Actually, it was all I could do." He was thoughtful for a moment. "I was glad to hear that you were involved."

"I'm not so sure that it was the smartest move I've ever made." Joe stared into his drink for a moment.

"Maybe not, but it was the right move. And the way things are going, you are this kid's only chance to survive. It may take a few days, but eventually they will figure out that Wendy is Charley's mother. There isn't time for me to bring in someone else. So, I'm sorry to say, you're it."

"It's not a problem. I made a promise to Wendy. And if I had any second thoughts, they disappeared when I met Charley." Joe refilled their glasses and smiled. "So, now what do I do?"

"Here." Fitzpatrick shifted around in his chair and handed him a cell phone. "This is a clean phone. It's already programmed with a blind cell number that will reach me anytime day or night." He paused, waving off a waiter passing a tray of hors d'oeuvres. "Don't even turn it on unless it's an emergency and you need to reach me."

"When you get back to the hotel tonight, don't charge your own cell phone, just let the battery run down. In the morning, go through your normal routine—workout, breakfast, conference calls, and all. But before you leave the hotel, pull the battery and SIM card out of your phone. They've been using the GPS feature to track you."

"It figures. I guess I should have thought of that possibility," Joe said sourly.

"I wouldn't worry about it," Fitzpatrick replied. "We're just too old to know all the latest technology."

"Who are these people?"

"We believe the primary opposition is a man known as the Bai Lang—literally, the White Wolf. He's the leader of a secret society that dates back to the Bai Lang Rebellion of the late 1800s. The organization became very powerful during the warlord era and the Opium Wars." He chuckled softly. "The English don't like to admit that they're responsible for the start of illegal drug smuggling in China."

"So, this Bai Lang still exists?"

"Over the years, the White Wolf and his army have gotten richer and more powerful, but they have always managed to stay in the shadows."

Fitzpatrick finally signaled a waiter. When he brought a small platter of hors d'oeuvres and placed it on the table, he whispered something to Fitzpatrick and moved away.

"Well, it seems that you are a very popular fellow tonight. The deputy minister of justice has asked to be seated next to you at dinner."

Joe was surprised by the request. "What do you make of that?"

"It should make for interesting dinner conversation."

"Okay." Joe brought them back to the issue at hand. "Do you have any idea who the White Wolf is?"

"No one knows, not even Chinese intelligence." Fitzpatrick stabbed a jumbo shrimp with a toothpick. "We do know that they are powerful and very well connected in the central government."

"What about the two guys who jumped me? Were the police able to question them?"

"Funny thing, the guy you hit came out of surgery okay, but someone injected a syringe full of air into his IV while he was in recovery. He never woke up." Fitzpatrick was grim.

"What about the other one?"

"He's dead too. Inspector Chou said they're trying to figure out what killed him. The bottom line is that we are no closer to knowing who *they* are, but we do know they're still after you. You're the only tangible lead they have, so odds are they'll keep coming after you."

"Terrific!" Joe drained the last of his vodka. "What happens tomorrow?"

"Take only the essentials with you when you leave the hotel, only the things you can put in that backpack. I'll have my people take care of your other luggage so that won't be a problem. Vicki has an escape plan she'll tell you about tomorrow." Fitzpatrick paused again, choosing his words carefully. "Look, you have to disappear for a few days. I can get all three of you out of China, but it's going to take some time to set up."

"How much time do you need and how many Chinese laws are we going to break in the process?" Joe asked resignedly.

"You've got four days to get to Shanghai. I'll meet you in the Dragon Phoenix room of the Peace Hotel on the Bund at three thirty next Friday afternoon. And, for what it's worth, we're not going to break any Chinese laws if I can help it."

At that point, the guests were called in to dinner, which was just as well as there didn't seem to be much left to discuss. As the two men followed the crowd toward the dining room, they were approached by a tall, elegantly dressed gentleman.

"Ah, Mr. Fitzpatrick, is this the famous Joe Wilder?"

"Joe, allow me to introduce Mr. Wei Yung-Chen, deputy minister of justice of the People's Republic of China." Fitzpatrick said with a gracious smile. "He was very concerned about you after your experience last night."

"It is an embarrassment when a visitor to China is attacked in such a way."

"Well, thank you for the good wishes." The two shook hands formally.

"I should very much like to hear about your adventure, Mr. Wilder." They walked into the dining room together. "I believe we are sitting together."

EiGHT

IT WAS A BEAUTIFUL, CLEAR, AND SUNNY DAY, WITH TEMPERATURES in the high seventies. The kind of day tourists love. Joe spotted the tail just as the taxi pulled away from the hotel. This time, he made no effort to lose them.

The courtyard between the ancient Drum and Bell Towers, a rectangular area loosely resembling a Roman circus, was lined with shops and restaurants that fronted on a perimeter road circling the square. The inside curb of the road was lined with bicycle powered rickshaws idly waiting for a fare to take into the hutongs—the old alleyways of the neighborhood.

Glancing back at the unmarked police car, Joe swung the taxi door shut and crossed to the center of the square. It was still fairly early. Only three buses were disgorging tourists at that hour. By noon, the square would be filled with tour buses as hundreds of sightseers shuffled between the towers. He slipped in with the first group that was heading toward the Drum Tower entrance.

A double staircase led up to the top floor of the tower. Joe spent a few minutes walking around the center drum display. His eyes moving continuously, cautiously examining faces from behind his sunglasses. Finally, after circling the drums twice, he spotted Vicki and Charley standing off in a corner.

"I think we're in the clear," Joe said as he approached them. "The police are still down below."

"Here, put these on." Vicki handed him a yellow lightweight nylon jacket and baseball cap matching her own. "We are Mr. and Mrs. Joe Thomas, traveling with our son, Charley. We've been on this Mandarin Tour for the last three days. Here's your tour pass."

"So, we're hiding in plain sight?" he asked, smiling as he put on the jacket and cap.

Joe hung the pass around his neck as the three of them slipped into the middle of the Mandarin Tour group gathered around their guide.

"The Drum Tower and its sister, the Bell Tower, were built in 1272 during the Yuan dynasty. Originally, there was one large drum and twenty-four smaller drums." She paused for a moment, letting the group absorb the information. "During three dynasties, the Yuan, Ming, and Qing, from 1272 until 1911, these two towers were the time-telling center of the city."

The guide, a tall, slim American blond woman in her late twenties, turned toward the terrace railing and waved her audience to follow.

"From the time they were built the area between them became a cultural and business center." She leaned over the railing to look at the square. "Some of these shops have been in continuous use since 1272." She turned back to her audience with a triumphant smile.

"Please take some time now to examine the drums and walk around the terrace. The views of the city are breathtaking." Then she moved back toward the stairs. "We will meet back at the bus in twenty minutes."

Joe stood at the terrace rail beside another member of the group. The man held a Nikon D7000 idly in his hands but made no effort to take any photos.

"That's a great camera," Joe said. "How do you like that 300 mm lens?"

"It's great!" He was only too happy to talk about his camera. "This thing can run continuous frames per second, or you can shoot video. And with this lens, I can shoot a close up from a mile away."

"Can I take a look?"

"Sure." He handed over the camera.

Leaning against the rail, Joe used his elbows as a tripod to steady the camera and focused his attention on the square below. Methodically, he panned the lens back and forth from the street in front of the tea shop, across the parking area, and back again until he spotted the plainclothes detectives. Obviously bored with their assignment, they sat at an outdoor table sipping tea and chain smoking. After all, there was only one entrance and exit from the tower.

"Thanks." Joe handed the camera back and checked his watch as he turned back to Vicki. The group had been in the tower more than an hour. "I think we should get back to the bus now."

At the bottom of the stairs, Joe scooped Charley up in his arms and held him like a small child.

"Curl up in a ball and make yourself look really small," he instructed.

"Why?" Vicki asked.

"They are looking for a man alone, not a family with a small child."

Vicki took his other arm completing the image of a young family on tour. The small flood of yellow jackets and baseball caps stretched out from the Drum Tower exit across the parking area and queued up at their bus.

Ten minutes later, the driver started the engine and the Mandarin Tour was under way.

From the back seat of the bus, Joe had a clear view of the two detectives scurrying around in a panic. The Drum Tower had only one public entrance and exit. As the last tour group vacated the tower, the detectives realized their target had disappeared, and they had no idea how.

"We are going to stop for lunch at a special resort near the Summer Palace," the tour guide explained. "They have prepared an exceptional traditional Chinese lunch especially for our group." She reached into the overhead storage compartment for a stack of tour brochures before continuing. "We'll spend the rest of the day at the Summer Palace. In Chinese, it's called Yi He Yuan, which means the Garden for Maintaining Health and Harmony."

"Her accent is terrible!" Charley muttered under his breath, trying not to laugh out loud.

"Shhh!" Vicki gave him an elbow in the side.

An hour on the road brought them to a beautiful five-star Michelin-rated resort. It turns out that the Jade Spring Hotel and golf club was hosting the Mandarin Tour group's luncheon. In designing the main hotel and spa buildings to function as the center of the complex, the architect had chosen a broad hilltop that gave hotel guests an extraordinary 190-degree panoramic view of the Summer Palace, the Kunming Lake and surrounding gardens.

"Remember your bus number and get back on the same one," the guide cautioned. "The other Mandarin Tour buses will be going to different sites this afternoon."

A steady stream of yellow hats and jackets, three busloads in all, were guided along the covered walkways and through the hotel lobby to the Terrace Restaurant.

"Please seat yourselves," the guide said. "The hotel has selected the menu today, so I hope you enjoy it."

Seating nearest the floor-to-ceiling windows seemed to fill up quickly as couples and family groups shared the open tables. Joe chose a smaller table for four a little off to one side. It afforded them an excellent view of Longevity Hill and Kunming Lake, as well as the main entrance and the kitchen doors.

Within minutes, an army of servers began streaming from the kitchen with trays of hot food. It was community-style dining, every table received bowls of steaming wild rice, shrimp braised in garlic-laced oil, and whole baked fish as well as steamed and sautéed vegetables. Several small round dishes containing a variety of dipping sauces that Joe couldn't identify were set before each guest. Pitchers of water and sodas were placed on each table as well.

"Be very careful, Joe," Vicki admonished with a smirk. "That clear sauce with the red and yellow things floating in it is very spicy."

The seventeen-course meal was designed to fulfill the fantasy of Western travelers visiting China for the first time. It wasn't gourmet dining, but the food was tasty and plentiful. As their meal neared its conclusion an hour and half later, the tour guide joined them.

"Well, it's nice to meet you, Mr. and Mrs. Joe Thomas," she said with a grin. "And this must be Charley. How're you doing, kiddo?"

She got a warm smile from the boy in response. Her name was Gail Warren, twenty-eight years old, born and raised in Bremerton, Washington. She'd received a graduate degree from the University of Hong Kong in Chinese history and was fluent in Cantonese, Mandarin, French, and naturally, English.

"Here are your receipts, ticket stubs, and brochures from our stops so far on the tour. Your names show up on all of our earlier stops and the hotels all have you registered." She slid a small sealed envelope across the table to Joe. "There's also an itinerary for the rest of our trip, including hotels." Gail smiled as she spoke, allowing her gaze to sweep the dining room occasionally. "From what Fitzpatrick told me, you may need to leave the tour at some point and rejoin us later."

"I hope that won't be necessary," Vicki said softly.

"When is the tour set to arrive in Shanghai?" Joe asked.

"Around twelve noon, Friday." Gail got to her feet and pushed the chair in. "I guess I should finish my rounds. If you need anything, just let me know."

"Thank you," Charley said.

"You're very welcome, Charley." She tousled his hair before moving on to the next table.

<hr />

THE YELLOW MANDARIN TOUR BUS WAS ONLY ONE OF TWENTY OR more buses parked near the entrance of the Summer Palace.

"We have a lot to see, so keep an eye on my flag." Gail announced as they disembarked. "If you get separated from our group, come back to the bus. There are uniformed park rangers that can give you directions if you get lost."

Once through the East Palace Gate, they followed the paths from the Hall of Benevolence and Longevity through Harmony Court.

"This is where the Dowager Empress Cixi held court and ran the government from behind an elaborate screen during most of her later years." Gail gave a running commentary on the history of each site as they moved from building to building. "Originally called the Garden of Clear Ripples, construction was begun in 1750. It was destroyed by British and French troops in 1860 and rebuilt by Empress Cixi in 1888. She renamed it the Summer Palace."

As they walked along the path, Gail pointed out that the beauty and variety of the plants and flowers had been specifically chosen by the designers to heighten the overall visual impact of the Summer Palace and gardens. When they entered the second palace, Joe realized that Charley had become a fixture at Gail's side. He seemed to have endless questions about the buildings, their history, and the antique furnishings.

"How much does Charley know about his family history?" Joe asked as they watched him question Gail about a particular bronze sculpture.

"Charley is a very bright, very mature kid," Vicki replied. "He knows the whole story, and he understands the danger he's in."

"What did you tell him about Wendy?"

"Only that she died protecting him," she said, sadly. "It's much more than any twelve-year-old needs to know."

By the time the Mandarin Tour group reached the Marble Boat, the sea of yellow baseball caps had become a long string of meandering stragglers. The Joe Thomas family walked along the path just far enough away from other members of the group so they couldn't be overheard.

"Fitzpatrick said that you had a plan. Is this it?" Joe asked, finally.

"It was the best I could do on the spur of the moment." Vicki wasn't sure if he was being critical or not. "Fitzpatrick needs four days to set up our escape plan. If we stay in one place, we run the risk of being spotted by the Bai Lang's people. But if we stay with the tour, we are constantly on the move. Besides, the only place a big American like you could go unnoticed in China is in the middle of a group of American tourists."

"It's a good plan. Look, Vicki, we have to assume that we are pretty much on our own until we get to Shanghai." He stopped for a moment to pull three bottles of water out of his backpack. Handing one to Vicki, he called to Charley. When the boy turned around, Joe tossed him the bottle like a football. He watched Charley snag the bottle on the fly and then run to catch up with Gail. "But I think we need to make some contingency plans in case something happens."

"HOW IS IT POSSIBLE THAT HE PUT TWO OF YOUR BEST MEN IN THE hospital?" The Bai Lang demanded angrily as he paced the floor of his penthouse like a caged animal.

"He was lucky," Lin Zhang Lei replied. He didn't like making excuses for the botched kidnap attempt. "Our people made a thorough search of the office after Wen Shu Xian jumped out the window but found nothing useful. All they brought back was her laptop computer and some meaningless files."

"How do you know this American knows anything that will help us? Why did your men go after him and alert the police in the process?"

"We found something when we hacked her laptop." Being the youngest member of the inner circle, Sun Wang Ji was the most computer savvy. "She gave this American a great gift by way of a new contract for the things he buys in China. And I think he helped hide the child in exchange."

"Where is Joe Wilder now?"

"In his efforts to elude the police, he has also eluded our people." Hsu Wang Ping, the great negotiator, commented. "But we will find him soon."

"Do it quickly!" The Bai Lang banged his fist on the table for emphasis. "We are running out of time. The Central Committee is meeting in four weeks. If I have that child in my hands, I will control the committee and we will own two-thirds of the Chinese economy. So, if you do not have enough people for the job, recruit as many as you need."

The Bai Lang abruptly left the room, bringing the emergency meeting of the inner circle to an end.

IT WAS WELL AFTER FIVE O'CLOCK BY THE TIME THE MANDARIN Tour buses were loaded and on the road again. Most of their group, exhausted from a day of walking the endless paths of the Summer Palace grounds in the bright afternoon sun and fresh air, slept or tried to sleep during the forty-five-minute drive to the hotel.

"Pick up your room keys from the tour desk in the lobby," Gail instructed as they disembarked from the bus. It was a smaller hotel in the Dongcheng district of Beijing and geared to the tour company trade.

"Your luggage will be delivered to your rooms in a few minutes." Gail was doing her best to move her group along. "Remember, everyone: breakfast starts at seven o'clock tomorrow morning. We are back on the bus at nine sharp!"

Although it wasn't a five-star inn by any stretch of the imagination, for a tour group hotel it wasn't half bad. Two restaurants and a good-sized bar opened off the larger-than-average lobby. There were several comfortable seating areas scattered around the lobby that made it convenient for tour-group members to congregate. It also made it easier for the Joe Thomas family to blend into the crowd.

"You two take the beds. I'll take the sofa," Joe said, as he tossed his backpack on the couch and pulled the drapes closed. Their tenth-floor room was larger than expected and furnished with two queen-size beds separated by a night table. A modern chest of drawers stood against the opposite wall and supported a large flat-screen television. An eight-foot sofa was pushed against the wall below the windows and behind a low coffee table. Without comment or explanation, he retrieved the scanner and made a quick check of the room.

"All clear," Joe announced.

"What is that?" Charley asked. Joe noted the confused expression on the boy's face.

"It checks for hidden microphones, listening devices, or cameras." He handed the little electronic scanner to Charley.

"Cool!"

"I wonder if they gave us bathrobes." Vicki slid the closet doors open and found four suitcases neatly stacked inside. "Look! This is my suitcase, and this one is Charley's, but how did they get here?"

"Our friend Fitzpatrick has been at work." Joe recognized his garment bag and carry-on from across the room. "I guess he had someone pack up my things from the hotel and he did the same for you."

"What about dinner?" Charley asked. "I'm hungry!"

"We'll order room service," Joe replied, pulling his garment bag from the closet. That seemed to please Charley immensely.

In keeping with the illusion of a typical American family on holiday, Charley ordered a cheeseburger, fries, and a Coke, while a salad with grilled chicken seemed to suffice for Vicki. Joe ordered and devoured a surprisingly good New York steak. By eleven o'clock, the dirty dishes were out in the hall, and the door was securely locked.

The television was tuned to CNN with the volume turned low while Joe tapped quietly on his laptop. Emotionally exhausted, Vicki had fallen into a deep sleep almost as soon as her head touched the pillow. On the other hand, Charley was restless, unable to sleep. Finally, the boy came over to sit next to Joe.

"Who are you writing to?" Charley asked, after watching the computer screen for a few minutes.

"I'm writing to my secretary in Los Angeles. Her name is Millie," Joe explained. "Without a cell phone, this is the only way I can stay connected to my office."

"Oh." He seemed satisfied and sat silently for a while as Joe finished writing, pressed send and shut down the computer. Leaning back, he stretched his arm across the back of the soda.

"What have you got there?" Joe noticed the boy was holding a small piece of carved jade.

"It's my dragon." He held up a beautifully carved piece of imperial jade four or five inches long and a little more than two inches in diameter. The carved dragon seemed to be climbing along the jade with one leg extending outward, its five claws spread wide and reaching up to grab something unseen.

"I think this is the same dragon figure that I saw in the Forbidden City."

"My mother gave it to me," he said sadly. "It was my grandfather's. She said the dragon's claw would always protect me." Charley seemed to be lost in memories for a moment as he leaned into Joe's side.

"Are you really going to take us to America?" His voice was soft and quiet as his fingers traced the lines in the jade figure. It was the sound of a frightened child in need of comforting not the outgoing preteen of earlier in the day.

"Yes, I am," Joe said, pulling the boy into a bear hug. "And as long as I'm around, no one is ever going to hurt you or Vicki."

After a long moment, Charley began to cry very quietly, sinking further into Joe's embrace.

"I miss my mother."

NINE

BY NINE O'CLOCK, THE EARLY-MORNING HAZE HAD ALREADY BURNED off, leaving a near-cloudless sky. A perfect day for sightseeing. The slight breeze coming from the east kept the temperatures in the midseventies, just warm enough to be comfortable without a jacket.

Streaming out of the main hotel entrance into the bright morning sunlight, they found four Mandarin Tour buses waiting to load passengers. Gail stood beside their bus, encouraging everyone to move along quickly. It took considerable organizational skills to separate the groups and get everyone on the right bus, but the Mandarin Tour had had many years to perfect its system. When the buses were fully loaded, the convoy began its ninety-minute trek.

"We have a very full schedule today." Gail waited just long enough for the driver to close the door and pull away from the curb. "Our first stop will be the Badaling section of the Great Wall." She paused again as if waiting for applause. "This portion of the Great Wall was built during the Ming dynasty, between 1368 and 1644. It is the most well preserved part of the wall and is listed as one of the Seven Wonders of the World."

Joe barely listened to Gail's spiel. He had moved their seats to the row behind the driver so that he could check the rearview mirrors. Their bus was second in line on the road, so he couldn't really see anything, which made him a little nervous.

Once out of the city, they drove for nearly forty-five minutes before leaving the freeway. The winding two-lane road seemed to narrow as the convoy maneuvered along to an elevation of more than thirty-two hundred feet. Gail kept up a running commentary about the passing scenery. Unlike most other tour companies, Mandarin preferred to begin the day at the Great Wall. As a consequence, the four buses arrived at the parking area ahead of the competing tour companies and the day's largest crowds.

"Everyone gather around for our group picture," Gail shouted, stepping off the bus. "Then we can go up to the tourist center. If you want to ride the cable car up, it will cost forty yuan one way or sixty yuan round trip, but I think you'll find it is much easier to take the cable car up to the watchtower and then walk back down."

The Mandarin Tours staff photographer, permanently stationed at the Great Wall tour bus parking area, hurriedly gathered them all beside the bus. Quickly arranging them in family groups, trying to keep the shorter individuals toward the front, he proclaimed them ready and took several shots in rapid succession before moving on to the next bus.

"The cable car will take us up to the number eight north watchtower," Gail explained as she led the way through the parking area with her band of sightseers strung out behind. It seems no one was adventurous enough to take the arduous hike up the wall.

"The views are spectacular from the north watchtower, especially on such a clear day. We'll walk back down the wall to watchtower number one. That's the Beiman Suoyne Pass and the main gate through the wall to Beijing."

Joe didn't like feeling so totally exposed. At one point, he wondered if this was really the best choice available.

Not more than fifty feet from the buses, the groups were besieged by a small army of street vendors selling a wide variety of tourist collectibles. Everything from silk pashminas and porcelain tea sets, carefully boxed for carry-on luggage, to sweatshirts proclaiming the wearer had actually climbed the Great Wall.

"You like pashmina? You pay ten dollah!" One vendor pushed the red silk material toward Vicki's face. Joe quickly stepped between them and put his arm around her protectively, pushing the vendor aside.

"No, thanks."

At the cable car station, Joe eyed the gondolas suspiciously as the four Mandarin groups merged into a single-file line. Although they only carried four passengers, the loaded gondolas seemed to swing precariously from side to side as they left the station."

"Are these things safe?" Joe asked.

"They sure look rickety as hell, don't they?" A pair of young college students, cuddling and holding hands, had gotten into line behind Vicki. Joe eyed them suspiciously.

"I don't think they've ever had an accident." Vicki returned the young man's smile.

"Well, that's good to know." The young man stood well over six feet tall, with blond hair, and sparkling blue eyes, and he had a warm, inviting smile and the toned physique of an athlete. He wore a sweatshirt proclaiming him the property of UCLA football. "Hi, my name's Jeff Winslow, and this is my girlfriend, Terri Cole."

"It's nice to meet some Americans," Terri said. "Our group is mostly Japanese tourists and there's no one to talk to." Tall and long legged, she had the lithe figure of a swimmer. Her blond hair was cut short to accentuate her pretty face and dark eyes that seemed to be in constant motion, taking in everything around her. Together, they looked like living ads for a California beach vacation.

"I'm Joe Thomas." With a degree of suspicion, he shook the young man's hand. "My wife, Vicki, and our son, Charley."

"Do you play football?" Charley asked.

"I played in college," Jeff replied. "But that was a while back."

"My mother went to UCLA." No sooner had Charley made the statement then it was their turn to board the gondola.

"On'y four people in each car, on'y four!" The attendant was adamant, while pushing them to hurry.

"But we're only three people," Joe protested, trying to keep the three of them isolated.

"Must take four people," the attendant insisted. "Look at long line. Take four!"

"Jeff, you go with them," Terri said. "I'll get the next one."

The gondola started off abruptly, jerking along the track. Once free of the station, they began an immediate ascent to the highest point on the wall. Although the ride up took a little more than eight minutes, the views became increasingly spectacular as the car climbed to the top. It struck Joe as odd that people were slower getting out of the gondolas at the watchtower end of the line than they were boarding down below. After all, the view was only from outside the station

"Move, please!" the attendants said repeatedly. "Meet tour group out on wall, please."

"I think I'll hang back and wait for Terri." Jeff said.

"That's probably a good idea," Joe replied, taking Vicki's hand and heading for the exit. He caught a brief glimpse of Gail from the station doors. She was waving her Mandarin Tour pennant in an attempt to rally her group.

"The Great Wall of China is a little more than thirteen thousand miles long with an average height of twenty-five feet. That includes the signal and watchtower ruins and the restored portions." Gail began moving along the stone path at a very slow pace. "In this section, it is wide enough for five horsemen to gallop along the wall side by side. Soldiers in the watchtower behind you were able to warn the other towers of an invading army."

"How did they send a message from one tower to the next?" Charley asked.

"Good question. They used a simple code—a combination of smoke, fire, or lantern signals and, in later dynasties, gunshots or cannon fire," Gail replied.

"Cool!" Charley was a true teenager.

"In fact, there is an ancient legend about the last king of Western Zhou dynasty. That was in the eleventh century BC. His lover was a sad, unhappy woman named Baosi, who never smiled. Hoping to make her smile, he ordered his men to light the beacon fires. When the nearby rulers saw the signals, they sent their armies to aid the king. When they arrived, the king said it was all a joke. Baosi laughed when she saw the faces of the soldiers going home. The king pulled the same trick three more times to make Baosi laugh. Finally, the northern tribe of Quan Rong invaded, but when the signal fires were lit, the other rulers thought it was a joke and didn't send their armies. The result was the destruction of the Western Zhou dynasty."

"The boy who cried wolf, right?"

"It's a slightly different story with the same moral."

Glancing around, Joe realized that although they had only moved some one hundred yards down the wall, their group had already gotten strung out and separated along the path. No more than eight or ten vendors were allowed this close to the cable car station, but some members of the group had stopped to examine the items being offered. Obviously, Gail was going to have a hard time keeping her group together.

"At the next turn, tower seven," Gail shouted, "there will be more souvenir hawkers than you have ever seen." She seemed frantic for a moment and then regained control.

"Okay, everyone in my group, please keep moving along the wall!" Gail shouted. "Take all the pictures you want, and we'll meet at tower five in thirty minutes!"

Joe watched as Vicki and Charley walked from one vendor to another along the opposite side of the wall examining their wares. To all the world, they seemed to be nothing more than a mother and son enjoying their tour.

This is what it feels like to have a family, Joe thought with a grin. *This is how it feels to really have a wife and son. This is a part of life that I missed.*

At that moment, he was sorry to have left the camera in his luggage. It was time for a reality check. Although they were a little more than a hundred feet away, it didn't seem to pose a security risk. Then he noticed a small Chinese vendor approaching with a bright-red sweatshirt spread across his outstretched arms.

"You like shirt? On'y fifteen dollah!"

"I climbed the Great Wall." Joe laughed as he read the printed shirt aloud. "No, thanks, I don't need it." He started to turn away when the little man jabbed something hard into his abdomen.

"Not so fast, Wilder!" The little man suddenly spoke perfect English. Joe saw the barrel of a nine-millimeter semiautomatic pistol peeking out from under the sweatshirt. The weapon was aimed directly at Joe's stomach. "You are going to do exactly what you are told, or you will die right here and right now."

Joe glanced at Vicki and Charley. They were all right for the moment, but he noticed another man further down the wall drop his carved wooden figures and start to move in their direction.

"What do you want?"

"We are all going to take the cable car back to the parking lot, and then we will take a little ride."

Seemingly from nowhere, Jeff Winslow walked up and put his big arm across the smaller man's shoulders just as the second man began to move in their direction. At five foot six, the gunman barely reached Jeff's armpit.

"Hey, Joe, are you trying to hog all the good deals?" Jeff smiled and turned his attention to the would-be gunman. "So, how much do you want for the shirt?"

"Go away before you get hurt!" The assailant sneered, pulling the shirt back to flash the gun. But Jeff just smiled and turned his attention to Joe.

"By the way, Mike Fitzpatrick sends his regards."

Jeff squeezed the little man's neck in the crook of his arm, choking off the blood supply to his brain. In that instant, Joe reached for the weapon, placing his thumb in front of the hammer to prevent it from being fired.

"You got the gun?" Jeff asked.

"Yeah, thanks for the help."

"You got another one on your six."

Joe spun around to see a second attacker some fifty feet away. Just as the man reached into his pants pocket for a gun, Terri crossed the pathway on the assailant's blind side, took three running steps, and leveled a vicious sidekick at the man's knee. The joint snapped instantly and he screamed in agony. A roundhouse kick to his throat silenced his cries and permanently ended his pain. Joe snatched the gun completely out of the first attacker's hand as Jeff slowly lowered the now unconscious man to the ground.

"Terri?" Jeff called out.

"This one's down." Bending over the lifeless form, Terri recovered the handgun from his pants pocket.

"Unh, Dad?" Charley's small voice carried the depth of fear gripping him at that moment. A third attacker, taller and younger than the others, had taken the boy. His left arm was wrapped around Charley's shoulder while his shaky right hand pressed a knife to the boy's ribcage. In an instant, three nine-millimeter pistols were leveled at this new threat.

"You okay, Charley?" Joe asked. The boy nodded. "Vicki, step away from the line of fire."

"He okay. He okay!" The young thug was visibly rattled as he watched Terri and Jeff move slowly outward, flanking his position. "You no do what I say, I kill boy!"

"You're not going to kill anyone." Joe kept his voice calm and nonthreatening as he took a few steps closer. "Vicki, I want you to translate everything that I'm going to say exactly as I say it. Don't change anything, okay?"

"Yes." Her voice was soft but strong.

"Now, here's what we are going to do. If you let the boy go and drop the knife, you might live through the day."

The attacker inched backward dragging Charley with him as Vicki spoke. Finally, with his back against the wall, he had no escape route.

"Terri?" Jeff asked from the right flank.

"I can put one in his right eye anytime."

"Vicki, tell him that the first thing I'm going to do is put a bullet into his shoulder," Joe said. "If it doesn't take his arm off, I guarantee he will never so much as hold a chopstick or anything else in that hand ever again." He closed the gap between them by a few more steps. "And by the time I'm done shooting away bits and pieces of his body, there won't be enough left to feed a dog, and I promise: he will be begging me to kill him."

"I let boy go, you no shoot me?" The young punk was pale, sweating profusely and terrified.

"Do it!" Joe said simply. The knife made a strange, tinny sound when it hit the ancient stones of the Great Wall. The frightened would-be assassin raised both arms above his head in surrender as Charley ran into Vicki's embrace. In minutes, Terri and Jeff had bound the two surviving attackers with their own belts.

Finally, standing together in the center of the pathway, as several frightened innocent vendors cowered against the opposite wall, Jeff addressed their situation.

"Joe, I think you need to get your family down the wall to the main gate and back on your tour bus as fast as possible." He checked his watch. "I figure we've got about five minutes before the police get up here."

"I guess you're right. Thanks for all your help." The two men shook hands, and then Joe turned to Terri. "I would have been in deep trouble if you hadn't covered my back."

"Anytime. I'm glad we were here." Terri smiled and gave Charley a high five. Then, as they turned to walk away, she added, "You realize the opposition is getting desperate?"

"What do you mean?"

"What does it tell you when two hard cases like these—and they have to be either ex-military or from some intelligence service—bring along a candy-ass street punk for backup? Hell, they didn't even give him a gun!" Terri gestured toward the prone knife wielder.

"Obviously, they knew that you were going to be on a tour of the wall." She continued. "My guess is they just didn't know which tour or which entry point."

"How does that make them desperate?" Vicki asked.

"It means there are probably other teams at various points along the wall, waiting for you to show up. To do that, they had to divide their forces to cover all the possible positions." Jeff added.

"So, they recruit some street toughs to fill out their ranks." Terri smiled. "And that says they're getting desperate."

"But the bigger question is still unanswered," Joe commented. "How did they know we were coming to the wall?"

They said a hasty farewell, leaving Terri and Jeff to explain the situation to the police, and took the cable car back down to the entry. Joe reasoned that they had already encountered the team set to ambush them at this point on the wall; therefore, retracing their steps should put them in the clear.

"We can wait on the bus until the rest of the group gets back." They watched as the gondolas carrying teams of uniformed police slid past in the opposite direction.

Once on the ground level, they joined the flow of tourists walking out toward the parking area. A number of uniformed police officers were milling around the cable car station, but they didn't seem interested in the Joe Thomas family.

"Walk slowly. Don't rush," Joe admonished. "We're just tired tourists who climbed the Great Wall."

They crossed the road and followed the walkway into the tour bus parking area. A white minivan parked beside the path seemed innocent enough until the doors slid open. Before Joe could react, he was struck in the chest by a tranquilizer dart fired from the darkened van. Within seconds, he was slumped on the ground. As consciousness slipped away, he wondered why Vicki was screaming.

TEN

JOE STRUGGLED TO OPEN HIS EYES AS HIS SENSORY AWARENESS BEGAN to return, accompanied by a throbbing headache that seemed to be centered in his temples.

I'm sitting up, he thought. *That's got to be a good thing.*

He tried raising his right hand, but the muscles wouldn't cooperate. The only movement he could manage at that point was sliding his fingers along the deep carvings on the arm of the chair. It wasn't much, but it was something.

"It will be a few more minutes before you are able to move, Mr. Wilder."

There was an intermittent metallic clicking sound that echoed in his head painfully as the man spoke. It was both familiar and disconcerting.

"Where are the woman and boy?" Speaking was difficult, but Joe managed.

"We're all right, Joe." Turning his head, he saw Vicki and Charley huddled together on a large Chinese daybed to his left. They were

107

frightened but seemed calm and unhurt. Finally, he was able to flex the fingers of both hands, stretching and then clenching them into a fist and releasing them again. At the same time, he stretched his legs out slowly and brought them back into position. He was relieved to know that he was not bound in any way.

"Who are you?" Joe turned to look at the man seated across from him. He was European, pale and slightly built. Since he was seated, there was no way to judge his height. He held a shiny Zippo lighter in his hand, opening and closing it rhythmically. At least the clicking wasn't all in his head.

"My name is unimportant, Mr. Wilder. It is my employer who wishes to speak with you." His English was tinged with a slight German accent. Joe guessed he was from Munich.

"All he had to do was call for an appointment. I think for now I'll just call you Heinrich." Joe could feel his body returning to normal as the tingling sensations slowly faded. "Who is your employer, anyway?"

"Oh, let's not play games, Mr. Wilder." The German laughed easily. "Haven't you guessed, a man with your experience? The Bai Lang is very anxious to talk with you."

As Joe turned in his seat. Two large windows. Double doors at either end of the room. A pair of smaller doors at the corners of the room were probably for servants' use. These seemed to be the only possible exit points. Joe estimated the room to be more than forty feet square. Thick stone walls and heavy timber construction didn't really tell him much. The walls were paneled in an old English style, while the stone floors were covered with beautiful Chinese and Persian carpets. The four armed men aside, the room was incredible even by imperial Chinese standards. It was furnished with a mix of traditional Chinese and contemporary European pieces. He was seated across from the German, separated by a low coffee table strewn with the latest edition of the *China Post*. Joe's backpack lay in the center of the table, seemingly untouched. A large rectangular rough-hewn wooden table was set up as a dining area across the room to his right.

If I can move, he thought, *I can take the German. What about the guards? Too many, and they're armed.*

Everywhere Joe looked, he saw exquisite examples of ancient porcelain, ceramics, carved jade figures, and bronze vessels of varying shapes and sizes. It seemed as if the room had been furnished from a catalog of exhibits at the National Museum. He flashed a reassuring smile to Vicki and Charley before addressing the German again.

"Where are we?" Joe asked.

"You are guests in the ancestral home of the first Bai Lang, not too far from Beijing."

The fact that he was so willing to speak freely didn't sit well with Joe.

"Funny, I thought we were in London." Joe hoped the sarcasm was clear enough.

"Actually, this house has a long and honorable history. As I understand, it was built around 1860 as a fortress to protect the surrounding village." The German smiled malevolently. "And it has all the accessories you would expect to find in any European castle from that period. Our dungeon is the equal of any in Europe." He paused for a moment and then turned the conversation back to the business at hand.

"We will have to wait a while for the Bai Lang. When they bring you food and water, I suggest that you eat and drink. The drug will make you very thirsty, Mr. Wilder."

At that moment, two women carrying trays of food and bottles of water came through the small door at the far end of the room. The items were placed on the long dining table on the other side of the room. Although there were eight place settings, the four guards didn't budge. As he got out of his chair, Joe picked up the folded *China Post*. Although he felt a little unsteady, he was determined not to let them see it.

"Do you mind?"

The German simply nodded his consent.

"Are we expecting more guests to join us?" Joe asked as they crossed the room. He held a chair for Vicki and seated Charley between them.

"Others will come shortly, but you should eat. Can you use chopsticks, or would you prefer Western utensils?" The German was being a gracious host, but the underlying threat was clear.

"I'd prefer a nine-millimeter." Joe fingered the slender tapered porcelain chopsticks. It seemed very elegant service for prisoners.

"Chopsticks it is."

Joe filled three plates with steamed vegetables, rice, and sautéed chicken. Vicki took the plate but barely picked at the food. Charley simply shook his head.

"The first rule in a war is to make sure you have the strength to fight," Joe said. The boy nodded and began eating slowly.

"I think we will have fun later, you and I." The German laughed as he left the room.

A little more than an hour later, after the remains of the meal had been cleared away, the German returned in the company of another man. Where the German was tall, thin, and pale, his Chinese companion was older, midsixties perhaps, short-cropped salt-and-pepper hair, heavyset, and stood no more than five foot six or seven. He wore an expensive dark suit, white shirt, and dark tie. Joe watched the man approach. His movements were heavy, lumbering, almost animallike in the way he crossed the room. He cracked his knuckles as he walked. Joe judged that he could move very quickly if the need arose. As the big man walked around the table, obviously assessing the three captives, an arrogant, cruel expression washed across his face. Standing behind Vicki, he said something in Chinese that made her cringe and the security guards laugh.

When he reached out to grab Charley by the arm, Joe seized his necktie at the collar and, in one sudden motion, jerked downward, slamming the man's head into the table. Before the security guards could react, Joe was on his feet pressing the sharper end of a porcelain chopstick against the man's throat.

"Please tell your thugs to put their guns away," Joe said quietly. "If I jam this through your friend's neck and into his brain stem, it will make an awful mess."

"You know I could easily kill you all." The German signaled the guards to back off.

"But you won't." He pulled the heavyset man away from the table and shoved him aside. If looks could kill ... The man glared at Joe for a moment before turning away. Returning to his chair, Joe dropped the chopstick on the table. "If you had permission to kill us, we would not be waiting to talk to your Bai Lang."

"I am afraid that you have angered my friend, Mr. Wilder." The German watched the man press a handkerchief to the red spot on his neck, muttering something under his breath to one of the guards. "He can be very painfully disagreeable when he's in a bad mood."

"I can be a real son of a bitch myself at times," Joe said and smiled amiably but without humor. "And just so we don't have any misunderstanding, I may be out of practice, but I will kill anyone who touches Vicki or the boy."

"Oh, Mr. Wilder, we are really going to have some fun after your talk with the Bai Lang." The German simply chuckled and leaned back in his chair, clicking the Zippo lighter. "But for now, I think my men will be safer if you are locked up for a while."

They were escorted through a windowless hallway and down a flight of stone steps leading to a basement of sorts. Joe guessed it was just below ground level and more or less beneath the great room upstairs. It was a large rectangular room, measuring some thirty by forty feet, with high, vaulted ceilings. In a different century, on a different continent, it could have easily passed for a dungeon. Aside from the stairs they had just descended, there was another set of stairs at the far end of the room leading to the upper floors. He counted ten doors evenly spaced on either side of the room. A guard opened the first door on the left and unceremoniously ushered them inside the dark cavern.

"Hey, what about some light?" Joe yelled as the door closed behind them. A second later, the single bulb fixture in the ceiling glowed dully. "Well, now we know the light switch is on the outside of the door."

"Is this some kind of jail?" Charley asked, looking around at the bare walls. The sparse furnishings consisted of a small round table with a single chair, a narrow steel-frame bed pushed up against one wall, and a small armoire.

"No, but if the German was telling the truth, in the 1860s, they built rooms like this to store food during the winter and in case of war," Vicki said dejectedly, sitting on the bed. "I guess the result is the same."

"What are they going to do to us?" Charley asked, the fear showing in his voice.

"I don't know, but if they wanted to kill us, they would have done it already. Instead, we're all waiting for this Bai Lang character." Joe tried to be reassuring. "That means we have some time to figure something out. More importantly, because we didn't get back on the tour bus, Gail will have notified Fitzpatrick that we're missing."

"How can he help?" Vicki asked. "He doesn't know where they took us."

"I don't know, Vicki, but so far, he's come through when we needed him. Besides, our family motto is *never give up!*"

"But we're not your family." Charley's voice had fallen to a whisper. When he looked up, his eyes were filled with fear and sadness.

"You became my family the minute I promised your mother that I'd take care of you." He pulled the boy into a bear hug.

"Does that include me?" Vicki asked hesitantly.

"Absolutely!" Joe smiled his most reassuring smile.

"Okay, so what do we do now?" she asked, sitting up with her legs crossed.

"Charley, do you know how to fold a fan?" Joe dropped the newspaper on the table in front of the boy.

"Sure." He seemed a little reassured.

"Okay, take about ten or twelve full pages of the newspaper and start folding them from the longest side into a fan—about a half inch wide for each fold—and press them tight." Joe thought it would be better to keep the boy occupied.

"What on earth are you going to do with a fan?" Vicki asked.

"We need something to use as a weapon, and a fan is a good place to start." He smiled again, but she still seemed totally confused.

Joe pulled open the armoire doors. The small hanging space above was empty; as were the three full-width drawers below. Pulling the bottom drawer completely out of the cabinet, he braced it on the floor with his foot and gripped the exposed end of the steel drawer slide. He jerked it twice until the thin wood splintered and gave way.

"At least now we have two weapons," Joe said, waving the two-foot-long steel shaft. He dropped it on the bed and carefully replaced the broken drawer in the armoire. With the cabinet doors closed, no one would notice the broken drawer.

"I only see one," Vicki said.

"How are you doing with that fan, Charley?"

"I'm done." He held up the fan-folded sheets of newsprint.

Taking the fan in hand, Joe pressed the creases tightly along the table and then bent the folded sheets in half. The result was an eight-inch-long paper club that was hard as steel.

"Jab this as hard as you can into a man's stomach, and it will rupture a spleen or tear the intestinal wall. Jam it into the small of his back, and it will rupture a kidney. Either way, it will cause a great deal of pain."

"How did you know how to do that? And what about that thing you did with the chopstick?" Vicki asked. "I don't know if I should be impressed or frightened. I thought you were just a businessman."

"I am," he said, grinning. "But I learned a few tricks along the way. Didn't Fitzpatrick tell you about me?"

She just shook her head.

"What now?" Charley asked. He was standing next to the door, running his hand over the smooth wood where a latch should have been. It swung outward into the hallway, and there was no way to open it from the inside.

"We wait," Joe said, checking his watch. "I want the two of you to get some rest. There's no telling how long it will be before the Bai Lang gets here. The German made it clear they won't bother us until then."

"I don't think I can sleep," Charley said, stretching out on the bed beside Vicki.

"I don't think I can sleep either." She propped her head up on one arm.

"You don't have to sleep; just lie down and rest. The second rule of war is that you can't win if you're exhausted before the fight begins." He tilted the chair back and slid one leg across the edge of the table. Vicki dropped back on the bed and closed her eyes.

"Do you have any kids, Joe?" Charley asked, staring at the ceiling.

"No." His smile carried a trace of sadness. "No kids."

As a boy growing up an only child, Joe's dream had been to have six children. His ex-wife, Carol, always said that she wanted children too, but it was never the right time.

"Oh." Charley looked thoughtful for moment. "Are you married?"

"Not anymore. We got divorced a long time ago."

Ironically, children had been the focal point of their divorce. They had met and married shortly after he'd started the company. It was a PR man's dream; the world-famous bodybuilder and the beautiful political analyst. Before long, WEI had grown into a multinational company and Carol seemed to be flying across the country constantly for one candidate or another. Finally, Joe pointed out that they—she—weren't getting any younger and that if they didn't start soon it might be too late. It was devastating to learn that Carol had continued taking birth control pills the entire time. The final blow to their marriage came with Carol's confession that she had actually terminated a pregnancy earlier in their relationship.

After a few minutes, Charley closed his eyes and fell into a light sleep. Vicky was already out. The fear-fueled adrenaline rush from the attack on the wall had faded, leaving them both exhausted. For Joe, it was an old familiar feeling.

He pushed the memories of Carol aside, focusing his thoughts on the problems at hand. What will he do when they come to the door? If he could overpower one or more of their jailers, where could they go? His mind was a whirl of what-ifs.

⌐✐⌐

ONCE THE PRISONERS HAD BEEN REMOVED, ONLY THE HEAVYSET man and the German remained in the great room.

"What about the woman, Max?" Lin Zhang Lei, the heavyset man, asked. "She is very pretty."

The German's name was Max Sterne. At least, it was his most recent alias. Born and raised in Frankfurt, the product of well-to-do parents and a string of expensive boarding schools, Max soon learned he had a fondness and talent for inflicting pain on others. A stint in the elite commando units of the German army completed his professional training in the art of killing. Three tours of duty in Afghanistan afforded Max the opportunity to perfect his skills as a covert assassin. Following military service, he sold his talents to the highest bidder. For the last ten years, Max had been on the payroll of the Bai Lang army, where everyone simply referred to him as the German.

Although Lin Zhang Lei spoke heavily accented English, it was far better than Max's Chinese.

"I thought you just wanted to kill Wilder?" Max handed him a glass of Irish whiskey.

"When the time is right, I will kill him very slowly and painfully." Lin Zhang Lei gulped the whiskey. "I think I will make her watch. But in the end, I will take her to bed."

"That will depend on the Bai Lang and what he plans to do with them."

"I can wait." Lin Zhang Lei refilled their glasses. "Where is he?"

"His flight from Hong Kong arrives in two hours. I'm going to leave for the airport now." Then, as an afterthought, he asked, "Do you want to come?"

"No, I think I will wait here." Lin Zhang Lei leaned back in his chair and smiled. It was a smile of pure evil.

"Remember: don't touch them while I'm gone," Max said, wagging a finger at Lin Zhang Lei on his way out.

THE SOUND OF SOMEONE TAPPING LIGHTLY ON THE WOODEN DOOR snapped Joe out of his light sleep. He glanced at his watch; it was just past ten at night. Reaching over, he gently woke Vicki and Charley. The tapping came again, followed a moment later by the sound of a key being inserted into the lock. As the door slowly swung open, Joe stood back a few feet, holding the steel drawer slide down against his leg, out of sight.

Two men faced him from just beyond the open doorway. They were dressed in work clothes and carried backpacks. Joe recognized them as two of the guards who'd witnessed his confrontation with the heavyset man earlier. The taller one spoke softly but urgently in Chinese.

"He wants us to go with them," Vicki translated. "He says there isn't much time before the Bai Lang gets here."

"Go where?" Joe asked. "They are two of the guards from upstairs?"

"Please—we are here to help you!" Stepping forward, the second man addressed them in English and introduced himself as Yu Tang and his partner as Wei Fong. He had Joe's backpack slung over his shoulder.

"These are yours." Yu Tang handed Joe the backpack and the Chinese-made Berretta nine-millimeter look-alike he'd taken from the sweatshirt salesman on the Great Wall.

Quickly, Joe pulled back the slide and chambered a round. Gently lowering the hammer to a safe position, he tucked the weapon into his waistband at the small of his back. Opening the backpack, he thumbed the loop of twine and was relieved to see the small piece of thread was still in place. At least the package had remained untouched, but the emergency cell phone was missing.

"We have to leave quickly." Yu Tang said. "The German went to the airport to get the Bai Lang."

"Why are you helping us?" Vicky asked. "Who are you?"

"As our fathers and grandfathers before us, we are sworn to protect the Son of Heaven." He pulled his right shirtsleeve up to reveal the image of a five-clawed imperial dragon tattooed on the inside of his forearm. It was identical to the imperial dragons Joe had seen in the Forbidden City. "We are the Dragon's Claw."

ELEVEN

THE TWIN ENGINE BOMBARDIER GLOBAL 8000 MADE AN impressively smooth touch down on the main runway at Beijing International Airport at exactly 11:28 p.m. The sleek executive jet made the run from Hong Kong in just over three hours, beating out the scheduled Lufthansa flight by ten minutes and thereby earning a priority-landing status. Turning left off the apron, the jet taxied toward the last in a cluster of six single-story buildings on the north side of the airport. The executive flight center was literally across the runways from the international passenger terminals and far away from the noisy crowds. Perhaps more importantly, it was out of reach of the layers of government bureaucrats that always seemed to be watching travelers with a wary eye.

Max leaned against the front fender of the big Cadillac Escalade while he waited for the Bai Lang to exit the terminal. The big, powerful American made vehicles had become the status symbol of China's new nobility—an extremely wealthy class of business entrepreneurs and high-tech moguls with a healthy appetite for Western-style creature comforts. When Max spotted his boss coming out of the terminal, he opened the rear passenger door and walked around to the other side of the black SUV.

"How was Hong Kong?" Max asked, sliding into the rear passenger seat beside his boss. The driver easily maneuvered the heavy vehicle through the sparse terminal traffic out of the airport and onto the freeway leading north of the city.

"Filled with endless committee meetings that accomplished nothing." The Bai Lang turned in his seat to face his favorite enforcer. "More importantly, what about our guests?"

"They are comfortable, but I had to lock them up in the dungeon."

"Why? Did the American give you trouble?"

"He threatened to impale Lin Zhang Lei on a chopstick." He briefly described the scene.

"Lin Zhang Lei must be very angry." The Bai Lang smiled. "He was both beaten and embarrassed. You must make sure he doesn't take revenge before I am ready."

"It's not a problem." Max said reassuringly. "He understands that you want time to question Mr. Wilder before he is touched."

"And what about the boy and the woman?" the Bai Lang asked.

"They are frightened, but this American seems to keep them calm."

"Good, I don't want the boy to panic at this stage of our plan."

It was just past midnight as they drove northeast on the freeway, circling around and away from Beijing. Even at that hour, there was a fair amount of traffic in and around the city. The driver managed to move into the faster lanes and push their speed up to eighty. Still, the Bai Lang knew, it would take nearly two hours to reach the village. They rode in silence for a time, Max in deference to his boss while the Bai Lang watched the passing scenery.

Once out of the city and beyond the suburban sprawl, traffic thinned to an infrequent vehicle in either direction. The surrounding landscape became more rural, more agricultural—mostly farmland occasionally interrupted by a small factory or industrial park. Eventually, the last vestiges of industrial development disappeared altogether, replaced by acres of cultivated land and occasional areas of raw woodlands.

Finally, as the freeway made a tight arch turning eastward, the driver took the next exit onto a narrow, two-lane paved road leading north toward the hills. A little more than a mile further they approached a cluster of seemingly dilapidated farm buildings that straddled the roadway. Two electric streetlights on either side of the street washed the area with a tint that barely eliminated the shadows. These were the only lights to be seen for miles in any direction. The big SUV slowed as it approached the pool of light. A single individual stepped out of the shadows as the big car approached. When he recognized the driver through his lowered window, the sentry waved him on through.

Another five miles down the road and the Bai Lang could see the lights of the village. It was a nineteenth-century fortified community perched on a plateau at the base of a mountain—literally a massive sheer rock wall soaring two thousand feet upward. The village sat at the end of a two-mile-long protective arm of jagged rock mountains, the result of an ancient volcanic thrust that had deposited the rich soil on the plateau and the valley below. These were the most productive and fruitful farmlands in the province. Even in the leanest years, the harvests were abundant and provided more than enough cash crops for the village to flourish. The Bai Lang always loved the view driving up the road toward the bluff. It meant coming home.

"Did I ever tell you that my family moved our entire village from the Henan province to this spot?"

"No, you never mentioned it."

"Back then, the village only had one hundred families. They built most of what you see."

"When was that?" Max asked.

"Around 1842 or '43, I think, sometime between the first and second opium wars. They named the village Yung-changzhaicun."

"What does that mean?" Max asked.

"Literally, it means 'the fortified village of the Yung-chang family.' We were one of the smaller warlord families then." The Bai Lang smiled, relishing how far he had brought the family business. "My great-grandfather was the very first Bai Lang. His name was actually Bai Lang. You know, there was a time when he commanded an army that controlled nearly all of northern China."

"What happened?"

"China was in the middle of a civil war. His army would capture a city, taking whatever they wanted, but give a little to the peasants. They said we take from the corrupt government and give to the people. Unfortunately, his alliance with Dr. Sun Yat-sen was short-lived, and he was killed in 1914."

"What happened to the family?"

"They destroyed our family tombs, our history, and tried to kill us all. They wanted to wipe out our family, but we got lucky. The communists were fighting the nationalists, so they were too busy to worry about us. We changed our name and went underground for a while. But we kept our hand in, and over the years, both our business and influence in the government grew."

"So, you are what, the fourth-generation Bai Lang?" Max asked.

"Since my great-grandfather's time, there has always been a secret Bai Lang and Bai Lang army. They call us Gelaohui—secret society. As you see, we have done quite well." He slapped Max on the knee and smiled excitedly. "But now, with this boy, we have a chance to seize enormous power, to take what should have been ours as spoils of war. With this boy, we can control the wealth of China from within the Central Committee!"

And I can finally avenge my grandfather's murder! he thought.

They continued on in silence, watching the landscape as they approached the village outskirts. The occasional farmhouse or outbuilding soon became a small town with workshops, stores, and a Buddhist temple lining the roadways. As they entered the village, the single paved road quickly became a web of narrow intersecting streets serving the needs of the town. In 1842, when Yung-changzhaicun was built, it housed less than two hundred families within the walls of the *Tulou*. As the community grew, the walled fortress was transformed into a palace for the Bai Lang, while the villagers built the surrounding town. Today, the population stands at well over six hundred families with two-thirds of these involved in farming and agriculture, while the remainder were dedicated soldiers and officers in the Bai Lang army—lucrative careers passed down from one generation to the next. While the Opium Wars had been a disaster for the country, they gave birth to the illicit drug trade and provided a seemingly inexhaustible source of funding over the years.

Originally designed to withstand a cavalry assault, the outer walls of the citadel loomed three stories above the roadway and were more than fifteen feet thick at the base. A pair of massive, bronze-clad wooden gates opened into a large courtyard and the eight steps leading to the entrance of the palace. Unlike many other *Fujian Tulou*, fortified villages in China, the Yung-changzhaicun was always intended to be a palatial residence for the leader of the Yung-chang clan—the Bai Lang.

Dozens of people were shouting and running across the compound carrying water buckets and fire hoses as the big SUV rolled to a stop in front of the palace. The front doors were open wide allowing plumes of thick, dark smoke to escape the building.

"What the hell is going on here?" The Bai Lang ran up the eight steps to the entrance. Once inside, he began calling for his chief of staff.

"I'm going to check the prisoners!" Max yelled over his shoulder as he ran through the smoke filled entry toward the great room in the north wing of the palace.

Two hours later, the situation was under control once again. They sat in the great room, and Max poured his boss a tall glass of whiskey.

"You will need this." He took a sip of his own drink before continuing. "The fire really didn't do much damage because it was confined to the security room off the main entry hall. Apparently, they soaked all the video equipment and recordings from the security cameras in two or three bottles of your best brandy and set it on fire." Max chuckled almost admiringly. "And then, just to make sure that we couldn't put it out, they locked the door to the room and broke the key off inside the lock."

"But why go to all that trouble? Why take the time?" The Bai Lang was confused. "Why not just run?"

"Isn't it obvious? The security tapes were the only pictures we had of the boy." Max pointed out. "Without a picture, it is going to be a lot more difficult to find him."

"And what about Lin Zhang Lei?"

"It seems he decided to ignore your instructions to leave the prisoners alone until you returned." Max paused, choosing his words with care. After all, he was a long-term ally of the Bai Lang. "He went down to the cells and dismissed the guards. I think that he intended to kill Wilder and rape the woman."

"What happened?"

"We found him sprawled on the floor near one of the cells. He was slashed open from his throat to his balls. It looked like he was attacked by some wild animal."

"How did this happen?"

"Traitors!" Max was grim. "Two of Lin Zhang Lei's guards helped them escape. I think they probably killed him."

The Bai Lang sat quietly, staring at his empty glass. Finally, he refilled their glasses before speaking.

"First, get someone to clean up the mess with Lin Zhang Lei. And then we must find that boy. Use everyone in our organization. Offer rewards on the streets. Someone will come forward. If you need to, put out the rumor that the boy stole money from me." He pulled a cell phone from his jacket pocket. "In the meantime, I will see if the police can be of any help. After that, we will deal with the matter of the two traitors."

TWELVE

As HE WATCHED THE SECURE ENTRANCE TO THE FORTIFIED VILLAGE recede in the distance, Joe couldn't help wondering if Yu Tang and Wei Fong had planned this escape route or merely acted on the spur of the moment.

Ten miles down the country road, the minivan turned east onto the G-6 Lhasa Expressway and picked up speed quickly. Joe took note of the fact that with very little traffic in either direction, Wei Fong was able to move to the fast lane easily and press the accelerator to the floor, pushing their speed to the limit.

"Please be comfortable," Yu Tang said. "We will be driving all night."

"Where are we going?" Joe asked.

"To Yinchuan," Yu Tang replied. "We need some help getting you to safety."

They took turns driving, pushing the speedometer to the 140-kilometers-per-hour mark. Somewhere around the halfway point,

Wei Fong pulled off the expressway and drove to a group of darkened buildings that straddled the junction of the expressway and a wide country road. The car rolled to a stop in front of a dilapidated wooden structure that could have been a garage. If they had been on an American freeway, Joe would have expected to see 7-Eleven signs and gas prices, but this rest stop seemed deserted. Nevertheless, he held the automatic pistol against his leg, cocking the hammer.

Wei Fong stepped out of the minivan and cautiously approached the door. He looked around carefully before knocking. As if they were expected, the big doors were rolled open, revealing a brightly lit machine shop and garage area. He exchanged a few words with the old man at the door and then returned to the car and spoke with Yu Tang.

"It is okay," Yu Tang explained, smiling. "The old man is Wei Fong's uncle. He will give us gasoline, and there is a toilet if you need it."

Relieved, Joe released the hammer of the pistol and returned the weapon to his waist band.

The pit stop only took fifteen or twenty minutes to complete, and they were back on the expressway. As the minivan settled in at 120 kilometers an hour, the steady motion of the vehicle, and the sound of the tires on the roadway had a hypnotic effect on the three escapees. Stretching out on the seats, they tried to get some rest.

Hours later, Joe had only managed a couple of light catnaps. He was restless, unable to really fall asleep and uncertain if the restlessness was due to his heightened sense of impending danger or the adrenaline rush he felt from the whole affair. Was it excitement or fear? Maybe it was just a renewed sense of purpose and anger—plain ordinary anger at the people who would threaten the life of an innocent twelve-year-old boy.

On the eastern horizon, the first light of dawn was slowly turning the night sky gray. In another hour, the sun would breach the mountain range and flood the landscape with bright sunlight and the promise of blue skies and a beautiful day. In that moment, their cover of darkness would be gone. The thought made Joe uneasy. It was one of those moments when he had no control over their escape, and he didn't like the feeling. He prayed their rescuers had some kind of plan.

Joe wanted to stretch, to move his aching muscles even a little bit, but that was impossible. At some point during the night, Vicki had stretched out across the seat and used his lap for a pillow. She was sound asleep, and he didn't have the heart to wake her.

The first rays of sunlight streaming through the window played softly across her face. For the moment at least, she seemed the picture of serenity. All the tension and fear Joe had seen when they first met was gone. At least for the moment. Vicki was absolutely beautiful with high cheekbones and large eyes that could be expressive, serious or mischievous one minute and guarded the next. A sudden urge to kiss her came as a shock to Joe. Resisting the urge, he gently brushed some errant strands of hair from her cheek.

What the hell did I get myself into? Joe thought.

He glanced back at Charley curled up in the next seat and knew the answer. The boy had wrapped himself up in Joe's jacket following their stop for gas. After a moment, Charley opened his eyes, looked at Joe, and smiled. Sitting up, he pulled the jacket tightly around his shoulders.

"Where are we?"

"We will be in Yinchuan soon, maybe an hour, maybe more," Yu Tang replied.

"Can we get something to eat?" Vicki asked without opening her eyes or sitting up. She was too comfortable, and Joe didn't seem to mind.

"We are meeting my friend at a shopping mall on Jeifang Street. We can get some food there."

"Good." She snuggled further into Joe's lap and seemed to fall asleep again.

THiRTEEN

THE VIRGIN LANDSCAPE OF THEIR NIGHT LONG DRIVE HAD LONG since given way to miles of cultivated fields on either side of the road, broken occasionally by tiny villages of no more than five or six buildings. As they drew nearer the city, they encountered clusters of small industrial centers. Frequently, Joe could see groups of factory workers gathered in courtyards between buildings performing a synchronized form of tai chi exercises. Their morning ritual before resuming work on an assembly or production line. Joe wondered if his products were manufactured in small factories like these.

Soon they were engulfed in the outer limits of urban sprawl, complete with wide boulevards, heavy morning traffic, and modern high-rise buildings that stood in sharp contrast to the narrow, crowded streets of the old section of the city. Yinchuan was simultaneously a university town—attracting students from around the world—a major trading center on the Yellow River and a developing industrial hub. For centuries, it had been the gateway east through the Great Wall into the heart of China as well as the empire's land access to the Muslim capitals to the west. The Silk Road at its best. As a result, the city's population of one and a half million people became a strong mix of Chinese, Middle Eastern, and Western ethnic groups. If you want to hide, to disappear into the crowd, Yinchuan was the place.

The white minivan maneuvered unhurriedly through the northeast quarter of the city, taking advantage of the morning rush. They still had two hours to kill before their rendezvous. The narrow streets choked with traffic that had characterized the older sections had given way to the broad, tree-lined boulevards of the newer parts of Yinchuan. Green spaces and parks neatly fit in and around the high-rise steel-and-glass office towers, hotels, and shopping malls. Known as the Phoenix City, Yinchuan was experiencing yet another incarnation.

Skirting the park and Beita Lake, Wei Fong drove leisurely south on Minzu Street. Even at this hour of the morning Joe saw dozens of small boats on the lake—people taking a quick sail before heading to their offices to start the work day. Finally, the minivan turned left onto Jiefang Street, moving slowly with the flow of traffic along the wide boulevard. The massive Bell and Drum Tower, a singular structure of gray stone walls topped with pagoda-roofed towers and resembling a medieval city gate, seemed to have been dropped in the middle of the roadway splitting the flow of traffic in either direction.

"What's that?" Charley asked. The boy had moved up beside Vicki and was leaning forward in his seat.

"That is the Bell and Drum Tower built by your ancestors at the beginning of the Qing dynasty," Joe explained and then pointed to the right. "That is the temple of the Jade Emperor. Your ancestors built that too."

"How would you know that?" Charley asked, his voice laced with doubt.

"Because I can read English," Joe replied with a tinge of sarcasm and pointed to a large sign describing the two monuments.

"The Double Joy Shopping Mall is just two streets down." Yu Tang turned in his seat and smiled. "Do you like McDonald's? We can get breakfast there."

Like so many of the modern shopping centers that have become common place throughout China in recent years, the Double Joy Mall was an immense horseshoe-shaped structure—a polished steel-and-chrome frame clad in dark glass, accented with brightly lit, colored neon signs and massive video screens to attract customers.

"Why do they call it the Double Joy Mall?" Joe asked.

"Because the address is 88 Jiefang Street." Yu Tang replied. "In Chinese numerology, eight is good luck, but eighty-eight—double infinity—is double joy. So, the developer named it the Double Joy Mall."

Wei Fong expertly slid the minivan into the only vacant parking space, not more than fifty yards from the front of the mall. Although the shops and restaurants didn't officially open until nine, another ten minutes, as usual there were crowds of people waiting for the electronic doors to swing open. Wei Fong said something in Chinese and then motioned them all out of the car.

"We should go inside now." Yu Tang nodded at Charley. "I'm sure McDonald's will be open for breakfast."

Joe noticed that Wei Fong stayed back, first watching his friends and then watching the crowd of people moving through the entry. He wasn't looking for anything in particular, just something out of the ordinary. Too much interest in a small group of tourists or a sudden fascination with a young Chinese boy. Fortunately, there was nothing to be seen.

The Double Joy Shopping Mall itself was a study in Chinese numerology. From the eight wide steps leading up to the eight sets of automatic doors that led into the mall, to the open-atrium lobby soaring eight stories above the ground floor and covering an area nearly twice the size of a football field. An enormous, domed stained glass skylight allowed the sun to filter through and wash the eight balconies ringing the lobby with a soft kaleidoscope of ever-changing colors.

Following Yu Tang, they joined the crowd streaming into the mall. Moving beyond the entrance, Joe was surprised to see Gucci, Chanel, Ferragamo, and Tiffany & Co. as well as a collection of other name-brand boutiques and specialty shops fronting on the lobby that would make Rodeo Drive envious. The stores were spacious, elegant, enticing and in sharp contrast to the small cramped shops of the ancient city streets.

They had reached the center of the courtyard by the time Wei Fong caught up to them. Yu Tang checked his watch and then slowed his pace, pretending to window shop.

"What's going on?" Joe asked.

"We are too early." They stopped near the entrance of the Le Printemps Department Store. "My uncle is meeting us at nine thirty, but I don't want to sit around the food court waiting."

"Another uncle?" They ignored Joe's comment.

"Can we go in?" Vicki asked, indicating the department store. "Charley and I need something clean to wear, and we could all use a toothbrush." Then she gave him an impish grin. "Besides, I have to get you something so you can shave."

"What do you think?" Joe ignored the dig.

"It's all right." Yu Tang pointed toward the food court. "Meet us by McDonald's in thirty minutes."

"Take this." Joe dug in the backpack and pulled out a wad of bills. "Only pay cash. They can trace credit cards." Vicki turned the yuan notes over in her hand and then gave him another mischievous smile.

"What size shirt do you wear, Giant or Panda Bear?"

"Very funny." He returned her smile. "Just pick out something in extra-large."

As Vicky took Charley by the hand and turned toward the store entrance, Joe nodded to Wei Fong. Taking the cue, the young man simply followed them into the department store.

More than a dozen restaurants lined the walls surrounding the U-shaped open seating area. Large ferns and potted palm trees were scattered among the sixty or more tables to add ambiance. Shoppers were presented with a choice of foods, it could hardly be called cuisine, from around the world. Traditional Chinese dishes, Mongolian barbeque, and Japanese shabu-shabu competed for customers with American-style pizza, hamburgers, and fried chicken. Even at that hour of the morning, crowds of people were queued up waiting to place their orders. McDonald's and KFC appeared to be the most popular.

It seemed to Joe that nearly two hundred teens and young adults had invaded the food court, splintered into small groups, and laid claim to a few tables, creating their own little enclaves scattered around the open seating area. After a brief study, Yu Tang picked a spot at the farthest end of the food court and pushed two tables together.

"How come there are so many kids here?" Joe asked, looking around with a sense of unease. "Shouldn't they be in school?"

"It's a local holiday." Yu Tang explained. "All the schools are closed today."

By the time Wei Fong, Vicky, and Charley had finished shopping, Yu Tang had managed to have a fair sampling of Egg McMuffins, burgers, fries, sodas, and coffee spread across the table waiting for them.

"I am so hungry!" Charley announced, dropping the two shopping bags in an empty chair beside Joe and snatching a sandwich. "We got you a shirt, but I don't think it's going to fit."

"Thanks," Joe said, continuing to slowly sip the scalding black coffee.

"There wasn't much to choose from in your size," Vicky explained.

"What else did you find?"

"A change of clothes for me and Charley, toothbrushes, toothpaste, a razor, and shaving cream." Vicky pulled the lid off a coffee cup and frowned at the steaming black liquid. "No cream?"

"It's hot and it's coffee. Don't complain." He passed her a sandwich.

"What happens when your uncle gets here?" Joe asked, turning his attention back to the problem at hand.

"He is coming now; you can ask him."

Joe looked up to see an older gentleman moving toward them. He was a heavyset man with a ring of salt-and-pepper hair surrounding a bald head. Walking with a slight limp, he carried a cane and favored his right side. The conservative dark suit and tie had been carefully chosen to exude an aura of financial success but without ostentation. As he approached the table, Yu Tang got to his feet. Following a brief conference in Mandarin, everyone was seated, and introductions were made.

"Joe, this is my uncle, Ai Tian."

"I am happy to meet you, Mr. Wilder." His command of English was excellent, but his pronunciation was heavily accented. "I have heard many fine things about the three of you." He said something else in Mandarin that made Vicky smile and Charley laugh.

"I have promised that you will get them safely to Shanghai," Yu Tang explained.

"And we will do so, but certain preparations must be made." He paused for a moment, glancing around at the other tables and then continued addressing Joe directly. "Now that the Bai Lang is personally involved in the search for you, it makes the situation more difficult."

"How is it different?" Joe asked.

"The Bai Lang and his organization either controls or has a finger in every major criminal activity in China." After a brief glance at Charley, he continued. "He has offered a very large reward for the three of you. Especially the boy. And since he claims that you stole a large sum of money from him, there won't be a drug dealer or petty thief who isn't looking for you." When Ai Tian leaned back in his chair, Joe realized he was scanning the clusters of young people scattered around the food court.

"So," Joe asked, "what do we do now?"

"I want to get you away from here and out of sight."

"Where?"

"I have a place nearby. It's only a fifteen-minute drive."

"Okay," Joe replied, but his attention was focused on a young man seated on top of a table in a very Buddha-like pose. He was surrounded by twenty or more high school and college students. Joe leaned forward, speaking quietly so that Charley could not over hear.

"Look over your left shoulder. There's a kid sitting on top of a table against the wall. Do you know him?" Both Ai Tian and Yu Tang glanced across the room.

"We must leave. Now!" Yu Tang quickly got to his feet and whispered instructions to Wei Fong before turning back to Joe. "He sells drugs to the high school and college kids for the Bai Lang."

"He's been very interested in us since you got here, and now he's on his cell phone." Joe stood up and grabbed his backpack.

"Wei Fong will get the van and meet us at the front entrance." Yu Tang snatched Vicki's packages and urged Charley to hurry.

Joe looked back at the Buddha-like drug dealer watching intently as they hurried away.

Mall, Joe spotted Wei Fong standing beside their white van and stopped abruptly. The young man was pinned against the van by two uniformed police officers.

"We have a problem," he announced. At that moment, a police car rolled up behind the van.

"Quickly, follow me." Ai Tian lead them to a black Mercedes S500 sedan parked off to the right of the entrance and well away from the van. Explaining the luxury car, he called it one of the perks of being a Chinese capitalist.

"What will happen to Wei Fong?" Vicky asked, a trace of fear creeping into her voice. Two more police cars arrived as Ai Tian pulled the big car away from the curb and merged into the light traffic on Jiefang Street.

"Don't worry. We have a few friends in the police." Ai Tian tried to sound reassuring without much success.

"But what about the Bai Lang?" She persisted. "Is this his doing?"

"I'm sure our drug-dealing friend from the food court is responsible," Joe replied sourly. "More likely, he called his contact in the Bai Lang's organization, and they called the local police."

"Most important now, I must get you out of sight. Then I can call someone to help Wei Fong."

Joe noticed that Ai Tian drove as fast as possible without arousing the eye of a traffic cop, working his way toward the river and the outskirts of the city. He made a number of turns and then doubled back onto Jiefang Street, finally turning south onto Qinghe Street. Another ten minutes and the big black sedan turned onto the G211 and then made the transition to the G20 Expressway heading across the Yellow River and toward the Yinchuan Hedong International Airport.

"Where are we going?" Joe finally asked.

"My factory is just past the airport." Ai Tian replied. "You will be safe there for a while at least."

"Does Wai Fong know about you?" Joe's level of anxiety was increasing by the minute. "I don't know how your police interrogate a suspect, but what are the chances they get any information out of him?"

"Not to worry, he will not tell them anything."

"Is that because he doesn't know or because he's too tough?" Joe persisted.

"It is because we know who will be asking the questions." Ai Tian raised his cell phone and dialed a number. After a brief but intense conversation in Mandarin, he ended the call. Then, glancing in the rearview mirror, he noticed Charley's expression.

"Wei Fong will be all right." But he didn't sound convinced.

A moment later, he slowed the car and turned left into the driveway of a newly built industrial park just south of the airport. The single building in the development was an impressive, modern, almost fantasy construction of steel, glass, and stone. It was a design more reminiscent of the sweeping architectural lines used for the Beijing Olympic stadiums than an industrial complex. A six-story-tall cylindrical structure, like the hub of a wheel, served as the focal point of the complex, with three long factory wings stretching out from the center like spokes. Each of the wings looked to be at least a thousand feet in length and three hundred feet in width. The wide, painted steel gate seemed to be the only entry through the razor-topped concrete wall that surrounded the entire park. A large sign etched into the wall to the right of the gate announced that this was the home of ATI MANUFACTURING COMPANIES, Ltd.

As the Mercedes approached the gate house, one of the four uniformed guards stepped out to check the visitors. Upon recognizing Ai Tian at the wheel, he simply signaled his partners to open the gate and waved them through.

"Impressive," Joe observed. "Is all of this your factory?"

"There are three separate factories here. We make several different clothing lines for American and European departments. Our jewelry factory makes high-end and costume jewelry for stores around the world. And our film division makes costumes, props, and special effects for the movie studios." He smiled proudly. "Actually, you could say I'm the chairman of a small conglomerate." Ai Tian parked in front of the entrance to the main building.

FOURTEEN

THE LOBBY OF THE UNUSUAL BUILDING WAS AN IMPRESSIVELY LARGE oval area flanked on either side by granite-topped counters. On the left, four young women staffed the twenty-foot-long reception desk, while the security desk on the right was managed by five uniformed and armed officers. Beyond the foyer was a wide hallway with elevators on each side and another pair of glass doors at the far end. Without making any introductions, Ai Tian held a hurried, whispered conference with one of the security people and a receptionist. A quick nod to Joe and he led them to the elevators.

"What's in there?" Charley asked, indicating the double glass doors at the far end of the short hallway.

"That is our showroom." Ai Tian replied. "I'll give you a tour later."

Access to the sixth floor required both a key and an authorized thumbprint on the sensor to send the elevator upward. The doors opened into a large living room with sweeping, curved, floor-to-ceiling windows overlooking the Yellow River and the city of Yinchuan in the distance. The room was filled with modern, European-designed furniture—lots of steel, chrome, dark wood, and leather—all turned to take advantage of the view. Off to the right, Joe could see a formal dining room, while the left wall was covered with photos, paintings, and low bookcases.

"Wow, is this your home?" Charley asked.

"No, I live in the oldest part of the city, but over the years we have found it useful to have quarters here at the factory."

Leading them further into the apartment, Ai Tian pointed to a hallway heading away from the entry.

"You will find a bedroom and bathroom down the hall. There are towels and bathrobes, please make yourselves comfortable." Then, almost as an afterthought, he turned back to Joe. "When you are ready, please come find me."

～ ✶ ～

"ONE OF OUR PEOPLE HAD THE GOOD SENSE TO CALL THE POLICE and report the van stolen." The German was amazed they had gotten so lucky. "Wei Fong is being held by the local police in Yinchuan."

"I want you to question him." The Bai Lang spoke without looking up. "Use all of your skills, do whatever you have to do, but make sure we get every bit of information out of him possible."

"You know Wei Fong doesn't speak English?"

"All right, take Chou Li Qing with you." He finally looked up and smiled. "He was Lin Zhang Lei's protégé, and I'm sure he will enjoy questioning the man who murdered his mentor."

"What about the local police? They may not take kindly to me questioning their prisoner."

"Li Qing has everything you need to keep the local police in line. They will do whatever you ask." The Bai Lang got to his feet. "I have to get back to Beijing. Call me when you learn something."

⟿

"ARE YOU HUNGRY?" JOE WAS STANDING IN THE DOORWAY. "WHY don't you join us? There are some people I want you to meet."

The living room was furnished with two long leather sofas, curved in a perpendicular angle to the windows and facing one another across an oval glass coffee table. Ai Tian occupied the single easy chair sitting at the head of the table. The furniture was turned just enough to give any guest the benefit of the view of the river and the city beyond. Platters of fresh fruit and sandwiches were pushed to one end of the table and a large city map was spread across the center. Charley sat between Vicki and Joe on one side, facing the three strangers on the other.

"Ah, Charley, I'm glad you are here." Ai Tian stood and began making introductions. "I would like you to meet Amy Yao. She is our costume designer."

She was a slim-figured woman, an inch or two taller than Charley in her bare feet, fashionably dressed in slacks and a silk blouse. Her stiletto-heeled, patent leather pumps with red soles were pushed under the table.

"Kevin Zou is our production coordinator." He was the oldest of the three, somewhere past forty, with gray hair starting to show around the edges. Tall and lean, he looked like a soccer player. "He makes sure that everything goes according to plan."

"And, finally, we have Tony Yang," Ai Tian said. "He makes the impossible possible. He is our special effects expert."

"Nice to meet you." He was a slight, bookish-looking man, wearing glasses instead of contacts. Standing beside Kevin, he seemed almost frail. He spoke with a trace of an accent.

"You sound English. Where are you from?" Charley asked.

"Born and raised in Hong Kong." Tony smiled. "English mother and Chinese father."

"We stole Tony away from the Hong Kong studios," Ai Tian added.

"What's going on?" Charley asked, looking down at the maps spread across the table.

"Our friends here are trying to figure out a way to make the three of us disappear," Joe explained. "Yinchuan is like the Hollywood of China. Ai Tian's companies make costumes, props, and create special effects for all the movie studios. Hopefully, they can use some of their magic to help us."

"Okay, since the Bai Lang has spies everywhere, including the police, it is too risky to try and keep you hidden," Ai Tian explained. "So we decided the next best choice is bring you out into the open and then make you disappear. The first act in our little play will be dinner at Uncle Robin's Italian restaurant tonight to set the stage."

"That's where I come in," Amy explained. "We are going to do this like we're making a movie. As the costume designer for this event, I'm going to dress you all accordingly."

"The idea is to draw out the Bai Lang's agents, let them see you, know approximately where you are, then have you vanish only to reappear tomorrow morning." Ai Tian spent the next hour going through the plans for the evening in detail.

"But what happens in the morning?" Charley asked.

"That's where I come in," Tony said. "We are going to set up a special effects gag for the benefit of our Bai Lang friends to make them think you are all dead."

"This is our jump-off point?" Joe asked, pointing to a spot on the map.

"Yes." Tony tried to look reassuring as he spoke. "It's an ideal site. The city is building a new bridge across the Yellow River, and they have three dredging machines working here." He traced a line on the map with his finger where the river curves nearly ninety degrees. "There's lots of activity, lots of workers, barges, and small boats. Plus, the water is relatively shallow. Our people should be able to control the situation without too much trouble."

"Okay," Joe said, "we get off the bus, join the morning workers, and walk along these two barges toward the big dredge."

"Right," Tony continued. "And when you're spotted by the police, you will have to run like hell to the end of the barges and jump over the side to the speedboat."

"Once you're over the side, you will be hidden from sight," Ai Tian added. "The police won't know anything until the explosion."

"Vicki, what do you think?" Joe asked.

"If you think it will really work, it's all right with me." Finally, she turned to Charley. "Are you okay with this plan?"

"I guess so." Leaning back in his seat, the boy smiled nervously. "How bad could it be? What's the worst that could happen?"

"Good!" Ai Tian ignored the question and checked his watch. "It's just four o'clock now. Amy, would you take our friends down to the showroom and pick out some suitable clothes for tonight and work clothes for tomorrow? I think six thirty or seven at Uncle Robin's for dinner."

"Better make it later." Tony commented. "The university crowd won't be there before nine. That's when the karaoke starts."

"This thing at Uncle Robin's is the hook. If they don't take the bait tonight, we'll have to abort the plan," Joe pointed out.

⌒φ⌒

THE SHOWROOM WAS JUST BEYOND THE ELEVATOR LOBBY——A HUGE semicircular room the size of a basketball court with twenty-foot-high ceilings. There were three rows of waist-high glass jewelry showcases some twelve feet long on the left and three dozen or more store mannequins arranged on risers running all along the walls of the huge room. Some of the figures were dressed in the best of European haute couture and the most fashionable ready-wear, while others wore extraordinary examples of ancient imperial Chinese costumes. But it was the six models dressed in police uniforms that immediately caught Joe's attention.

Row after row of clothing-filled rolling racks were scattered around the room, while the center was dominated by four large desks arranged like dominos facing one another. Each was manned by a young woman engrossed in multitasking between their telephone head set and the desktop computers. A dozen floor staff were running papers from the order desk out through the three archways leading away from the showroom. No one paid any attention to the new arrivals.

"This is incredible," Joe said. "Do you manufacture all these things?"

"Impressive, isn't it?" Amy said, smiling. "As you can see from the showcases, we make fine jewelry with precious and semiprecious stones for our catalog sales. In our clothing factory, we make a full line of ready-to-wear and custom designs—from formal to sportswear. We do our own designs as well as private-label work for some of the biggest department stores in the US and Canada."

"I couldn't help but notice." Joe pointed to the mannequins on the right. "What's with the uniforms?"

"Oh, that." Amy laughed. "We make uniforms for most of the police departments in Western China. It has been a never-ending source of information."

"What kind of clothes are these?" Charley had found two racks of clothes and shoes pulled away from the rest.

"Those are period costumes for a movie about the first emperor of China. Your ancestor," Amy explained. "We make all the costumes for the movie studios here."

"Until today, I didn't know there were movie studios this far west," Vicki said.

"Sure, Yinchuan is home to four of the largest movie and television studios in China." Amy paused for a moment. "That's why it was so important for us to get Tony to join us. There is nothing he can't do."

Amy led them to one of the desks and spoke with the woman quietly. Gesturing toward her guests, she explained the situation and brought the woman around to make the necessary introductions. Li Min was older than she appeared from a distance sitting at her desk. Standing no more than five feet tall with straight, dark hair cut in a short bob, she was a tiny, almost frail-looking woman in her late forties. She had a sour, disconcerting expression on her face as she walked around Joe sizing him up before turning her attention to the other two.

"They won't be a problem." Addressing Amy, Li Min waved a hand toward Charley and Vicki, preferring not to use names. "We have clothes that will fit the big one, but we have to alter them. How dressy you want to be?"

"We are going to Uncle Robin's at nine o'clock."

"Oh, you like karaoke?" she asked Charley, her face brightening momentarily with a friendlier expression, then continued without waiting for an answer. "We can make you stand out in the crowd or look like tourists." She finally smiled. "So, you want to blend in or you want to be noticed?"

Joe finally spoke up. "I think we want to be noticed. But we don't want to seem too eager."

"Okay, I know. I know!" Li Min called over two of the floor staff and held a quick conference while gesturing toward Joe. Finally, finished with her instructions, she sent the young men off and turned her attention back to the group.

"No worry. I make you look good." Turning her attention to Charley, she smiled again. "For you, I think we make you a teenager American style with Levi's and a sport shirt."

"And, now, what we going to do for you?" She eyed Vicki carefully, assessing her tall, slim figure. "You want Chinese style or American style?"

"Since we are supposed to be an American family on vacation, I guess it should be American style."

"I think maybe a pant suit," Li Min said thoughtfully. "Maybe you need to move quickly, so no skirt and no dress."

At that point, the two floor runners returned with their arms loaded with clothes. One held a selection of men's sport coats, slacks and dress shirts, while the other carried several pairs of Levi's and colorful shirts. An older white haired tailor followed closely behind them mumbling something in Mandarin.

"Ah, good, good." Li Min quickly flipped through the sport coats, then directed the tailor to take Joe to fitting room number one. She pulled two of the colorful short sleeved sport shirts out of the arms of her second stock runner and held each in turn up against Charley's chest.

"Maybe you try these two first and see what you think, okay?" She smiled reassuringly. "And maybe you take Levi's that are just a little bit big too."

She sent them off to fitting room number two before turning her attention to Vicki and Amy.

"I think I have something of my own to wear." Amy said.

"Okay, let us see what we have for you." Li Min led them off to a group of rolling racks on the right side of the showroom. She began flipping through a group of designer suits and dresses, searching for something specific. "Don't want to be too dressy, but same time, you have nice figure to show off."

Finally, she found an Armani-style red blazer and black slacks that were the right size. Li Min held the blazer up to Vicki and eyed the result for a moment before grunting approvingly.

"Now, we need shoes." She turned toward away from the two women and gestured for them to follow. "What size are you?"

"American or European?" Vicki asked.

"American." Li Min led them through the archway into a small shoe warehouse. Dozens of shoe racks created an intricate pattern of aisles with a rectangular clear space in the center of the room where two rows of folding chairs were arranged facing each other.

"Size six."

"Good, good. Now do we want low heel or high?"

"I think a low heel is better," Amy commented. "Just in case something unexpected comes up."

In response, Vicki simply shrugged her shoulders. Li Min smiled and gave quick instructions to the stock boy. Within minutes, the young man returned with six pairs of shoes and followed them to a dressing room.

After going through the pile of alternatives, they had chosen a black-and-white-houndstooth, three-button sport coat, charcoal-gray slacks, and a white dress shirt. The slacks had been simple, but it took the old tailor nearly an hour of opening seams and repining fabric to make the coat fit. At that, he was essentially going to remake the garment.

"How long will it take?" Joe asked.

"Not long, maybe one hour," the tailor replied. "I will bring everything upstairs to you."

The old man directed Joe to a small beauty salon just off the main showroom. He found Vicki seated before a large mirror where a young woman was putting the finishing touches to her hair and makeup.

"Well?" When Vicki saw him standing at the door, she got to her feet and did a slow pirouette. "How do I look?"

"Wow!" Her shoulder-length hair was parted in the middle, the soft waves cascading downward framing her face. Vicki needed very little makeup, just a little lipstick and some eye shadow to accent the natural sparkle in her eyes. The tailored jacket and slacks emphasized her slim figure and long legs. All in all, the effect was striking. Once again, he was struck by her beauty. "You look like a movie star!"

"Thank you," she said. "But what about you? You haven't changed."

"Oh, it will take them another hour to make everything fit." He said smiling. "Where's Charley?"

"With Amy, they're looking at jewelry in the showroom."

They found the two would-be shoppers had bypassed the diamond, ruby, and emerald showcases, choosing instead to focus their attention— at least Charley's attention—on some small carved pendants.

"Hey, Joe, look at these things!" Charley said as they approached. "Do you know what they are?"

"We've been making them for years for a Brazilian jewelry store, but I don't know much about the history of the design," Amy explained.

"That's easy." Joe looked at the two dozen or so pendants displayed in the velvet lined tray. Pieces of red, pink, black, and orange coral, along with chunks of imperial jade, were beautifully carved into figures one to three inches long depicting a clenched fist and forearm with the thumb inserted between the middle and index fingers. A gold bezel with a small loop for a chain, capped the top of each figure. He picked up a piece of imperial jade, holding it in his open palm.

"In Brazil, it's called a *figa*. It wards off evil, protects the wearer from harm, and brings good luck."

"We could use some good luck." Vicki picked up a rich reddish-pink coral pendant and held it thoughtfully for a moment before replacing it in the tray with a sigh.

"Which is your favorite?" Joe asked.

"The dark pink one, I guess," she said softly, momentarily lost in thought.

"Okay." She snapped out of her reverie, took Charley by the hand, and began walking away without waiting for Joe. "Let's go back upstairs. We have a lot to do."

FIFTEEN

By eight thirty, Joe was dressed in his new jacket and slacks. The tailors had done an excellent job of concealing the shoulder holster beneath his left arm. After inspecting his reflection in the full-length mirror, he took a deep breath, exhaled, and turned toward the living room to join the rest of the group.

"Hi, Joe." Charley was the first to notice his arrival.

"Wonderful, wonderful." Ai Tian rubbed his hands together. "Now that we are all here, we can get our little show on the road as they say."

"I found this on my bed." Smiling at Joe, Vicki toyed with the dark pink, coral figa on a gold chain around her neck. "It was very kind of you."

"I thought it suited you." He returned her smile. "Besides, Amy made me a good deal."

"Thank you." She put her arms around his neck, giving him a warm hug.

"Joe, are you sure boys are supposed to wear these things?" Charley sounded doubtful, fingering the small, carved jade figure.

"Hey, some of the toughest soccer players in Brazil wear one just like yours." He squared the boy's shoulders, standing him up straight. "Anyway, it's imperial jade, and you're the emperor."

"Come, come." Ai Tian was anxious to get them moving. "The cars are waiting."

Three black Mercedes S550 sedans were parked in front of the building. Tony explained the advantage of using three identical cars to make their exit from Uncle Robin's later in the evening. As he put it, a confusing escape was usually the safest.

The small convoy worked its way through the evening traffic and across the Yellow River toward the university district. The cars slowed down somewhere between Ningxia University and the Northern Minorities University as they approached a wood-sided building with a red awning. The white lettering announced in English that they had arrived at Uncle Robin's Pizza Restaurant. A few young people, probably college students, were gathered around the entrance either just leaving or waiting for a chance to get into the famous pizzeria.

A construction site directly across the street that was crowded with vehicles during the day, provided an ideal parking area for the three Mercedes at that hour of the evening. Two of the cars pulled in head first close to the fence, allowing the third car to back in and park between them. When Joe questioned the maneuver, Tony explained that they could open the rear doors of all three cars and move from one to the other while the open doors and dark-tinted windows would screen them from view.

"In the end," Tony said, "no one will know which car you are in when we leave."

"Cute!" Joe was impressed by the simple ingenuity of the idea.

"I think we need to go in now." Leaving the drivers to stay with the vehicles, Ai Tian led the small group across the street.

As usual, the twelve or fifteen small tables in the front room were crowded with diners. They were immediately enveloped in the aroma of fresh pizza, garlic toast, burgers, and fries.

"Good evening." The hostess greeted Kevin as if they were old friends. "We've been expecting you." He made the introductions quickly and quietly.

"Sarah is an exchange student from Canada."

She led them toward the back of the restaurant, through an arched doorway, and into the large, rectangular dining room next door to the original restaurant. The front wall consisted of a pair of large showroom windows, separated by a glass door that looked onto the street. Most of the two dozen tables were set up for parties of two or four people with nearly half already occupied. Sarah guided them to three tables that had been pushed together along the side wall to accommodate their group of seven. From this vantage point, Joe had a clear view of the former store front entrance, the archway to the main restaurant, as well as the kitchen doors and small stage set up at the back of the room. Impressed, he wondered if the placement was accidental or by design.

"Originally, this was a music store. Uncle Robin took it over about a year ago when they went out." Ai Tian explained once they were seated. "In the beginning, it didn't go well at all. Robin hired extra students to serve customers, but no one came. Finally, one night an American brought his guitar to work. Since he had nothing to do, he started to play. By the end of the evening, the room was full of people singing and ordering food."

"That's quite a story," Joe commented.

"It was great," Kevin added. "It got to the point where Robin had to put in the stage, a karaoke machine, and a couple of microphones. There is always someone who wants to sing or play music. Anyone can go up on stage."

As if on cue, a tall, blond young man mounted the stage, pressed some buttons on the karaoke machine and began singing a Beatles song in French, to the delight of the crowd.

Over the next two hours, the room filled to overflowing. While they consumed several pizzas, a chicken parmesan, two chopped salads, and countless breadsticks, individuals and groups of singers took their turns on stage performing in a variety of languages. Some were good, some great, and some painful to hear, but the crowd cheered them all. Charley seemed to get lost in the enthusiasm of the evening, enjoying the performers and the audience, even singing along to some of the songs. He deserved a carefree evening, Joe thought, worried that there might not be many more. Still, he periodically scanned the jam-packed throng looking for any potential threat and grateful that he found none.

"I think it is time." Tony Yang nudged Ai Tian and tapped his wristwatch.

"What about the bill?" Joe asked.

"It's been handled," Ai Tian replied and got to his feet.

As Joe's group worked their way between the tables, a young Chinese couple sitting toward the far side of the room quietly got to their feet, slipped the waiter some cash, and followed the group toward the exit.

A light rain had started to fall as they emerged from the famed pizza parlor. It was little more than a drizzle, but the drivers were already out of the vehicles opening all the doors. The seven passengers separated as they sprinted across the street, entering different vehicles and moving unseen from one to another. In a matter of minutes, the three black sedans pulled away from the parking area and sped off in different directions. The young couple could do little more than watch.

SARAH REACHED FOR HER CELL PHONE AND PRESSED A NUMBER ON her speed dial. When Kevin answered, she tried to speak softly in spite of the noise level in the restaurant.

"You were right, a man and a woman followed you out." She chuckled softly. "When you drove off, they didn't know what to do. It was kinda funny."

"Thanks, Sarah, I owe you," he said and ended the call.

AFTER LEAVING UNCLE ROBIN'S, THE DRIVER WASTED LITTLE TIME getting the sleek black sedan out of the university district. Once he was certain they weren't followed, he headed into the oldest section of Yinchuan. Most of the streets were narrow and poorly lit, stone and masonry buildings slowly giving way to wooden structures.

It was nearly midnight when the car carrying Charley, Vicki, Joe, and their host finally stopped in front of an alley in the center of the old city. The driver wished them good luck as they slid out of the car.

"We have to walk the rest of the way." Ai Tian smiled reassuringly as he spoke, leading them into the passageway. "It isn't far, but at least it stopped raining for the moment."

As they walked, the alley narrowed down to a walkway that was little more than a wide separation between the three-story buildings on either side and, finally, into the next street that was wider and completely hidden from the drop-off point. Turning to the right, Ai Tian picked up the pace, periodically glancing back to make sure Charley and Vicki were all right.

Out of an abundance of caution, Joe drew the pistol and cocked the hammer. He held it out of sight as they walked.

"Not many people live in this neighborhood anymore, mostly just old people now. It's very busy during the day, but at night it's nearly deserted." He kept looking around hoping not to see anyone. "I will feel better when we are completely out of sight."

At the end of the block, they crossed a small side street and then followed an old, ten-foot-high brick-and-stone wall for another hundred yards. A single, small light fixture mounted on the wall spread a dim pool of light around the only opening. When they reached the heavy, weathered wooden gate, Ai Tian stopped, lifted the latch, and pushed it open.

"Quickly!" He ushered them into the enclosed courtyard and then shut and locked the gate behind them.

The courtyard was entirely paved with unevenly set stones broken by two small flowerbeds placed against the walls on either side. A pathway marked by differently colored stones led to the entrance of a pair of very old, two-story wooden buildings connected in the center by a single-story structure. Eight heavy columns separated by large flat panel segments formed the facade of the first floors with a similar second floor portico, each topped with a pagoda-style tile roof. The panels might have been decorated with painted murals at some point in time, but now they were just a faded reddish color. Small floodlights mounted along the first-floor eaves illuminated the courtyard. It wasn't brightly lit, but it served the purpose.

"You are late; I was beginning to worry." An older gentleman, short and reed thin, dressed in a suit and tie, stepped out of the shadows once the gate was secured.

"I'm sorry. We had to be sure we were not followed," Ai Tian replied and then turned to the group to make introductions. "Mr. Gao is the caretaker here."

"Where are we?" Joe asked as he released the hammer and holstered the weapon.

"I'll explain once we're inside."

They followed Mr. Gao through the main entrance in the center building and into a small foyer. Large, open archways led into the main buildings on either side, benches lined the walls with a single door opposite the entry.

"They are waiting for us in the library." He led them through the single door, along a hallway to the end of the building and down two flights of stairs to the basement.

The library was a large room with floor-to-ceiling bookshelves lining the walls. Several smaller seating areas more or less surrounded a round table and ten chairs in the center of the room. They found the rest of their escape team, Amy, Tony, and Kevin, waiting for them.

Sitting around the table, they talked for a while, until Tony looked at his watch and announced the need to call it a night.

"There are bedrooms down the hall," Mr. Gao said, "and a small kitchen through the door on the right if you need anything. I will be here early in the morning to help."

It took a little time to sort out the sleeping arrangements. Once everyone was settled, Ai Tian offered Joe a glass of brandy as the two men sat together in the library.

"This is really good."

"A friend sent it to me from Paris." Ai Tian held his glass up to the light to examine the amber liquid. "This bottle is one hundred and fifty years old."

The two men sat in silence for a moment, each lost in his own thoughts.

"Are you ready for tomorrow?" Ai Tian asked.

"The more important question is, are your people ready?" Joe sipped the brandy. "Do you think this plan will really work?"

"Not to worry, my people are very, very good." He smiled reassuringly.

"What if it goes bad? Is there a plan B?" Joe could see every possible glitch in the plan, but he couldn't see an alternative either.

"All we have to do is buy you some time—just make you disappear for a few days so you can get to Shanghai. And, yes, this will do the job."

"From your mouth to God's ear!" Joe held up his glass in a toast.

"Well, this is the house for it." Ai Tian laughed softly.

Joe looked at the floor-to-ceiling shelves overflowing with books, stacks of soft cover pamphlets and magazines, small groupings of chairs scattered around the room.

"Where are we?" he finally asked, swallowing the last of his brandy.

"My friend, you are sitting in the library of the oldest Jewish synagogue in all of China." Ai Tian smiled broadly. "It was originally built in 1100, but over the centuries it has been destroyed and rebuilt many times."

"I thought the Jews only came to China at the start of World War II."

"Not at all, my family history goes back to the Tang dynasty, around the year 618. We have served the emperors of every dynasty since and in many capacities from ministers in the government to officers in the Imperial Guard, a position which is passed down from father to son, by the way."

Ai Tian rolled up his right sleeve exposing the tattoo on his right forearm. "Governments may come and go but, here in China, the Dragon's Claw will always protect the Son of Heaven."

〜〜

SUSPECT INTERVIEW ROOMS IN POLICE STATIONS THE WORLD OVER are fairly similar. One or two chairs, with or without a table, and a one-way mirror in order to observe suspects without their knowledge. In this particular room in Yinchuan police headquarters, there was a single metal chair bolted to the concrete floor and no other furniture.

The German ignored the three detectives sitting nearby as he watched Chou Li Qing interrogate the suspect. After all, this traitor was the only lead they had to find the boy. Their credentials gave them absolute authority to do as they pleased anywhere in the city and the Yinchuan police were too frightened to challenge them. Wei Fong was handcuffed to the chair, but it really didn't matter. He was in no condition to move, much less resist his questioner. Aside from various facial lacerations, a broken jaw and nose, eyes swollen shut, and several broken teeth, his thumbs had been broken early on in the inquiry. When he lost consciousness for the third time, the Bai Lang's chief enforcer finally left the room.

"He can tell us nothing more," Chou Li Qing said in English.

"It doesn't matter," Max replied. "I think we have what we need."

On Max's signal, two of the detectives rushed into the room to check the prisoner while the third called for medical assistance. Wei Fong was pronounced dead by the police doctor at two o'clock that morning.

SiXTEEN

THE YINCHUAN POLICE HAD SET UP A COMMAND POST ON THE ROOF of a two-story warehouse just above the service road. From this vantage point, they had a panoramic view of the entire construction area. It was nearing seven in the morning when Max and Chou Li Qing joined the chief of the Yinchuan security service on the rooftop. He was a heavyset man of medium height with a great appreciation for Italian food and a great distrust of people interfering with his department.

"How do you know these people will be here?" the chief asked.

Max knew the man resented turning over control of his police force to a foreigner without knowing why. But at the end of the day, the fact they had direct authority from Beijing was a frightening message to the chief.

"They will come because they have no choice." There was an unmistakable certainty in Max's voice. He could feel the slow adrenaline rush began as he imagined taking the boy back to the Bai Lang. "And remember: tell your people there is to be no shooting! I want them alive and unharmed—especially the boy."

"You said they have already killed two people. I have a hundred police here, and I won't let you put them in danger."

Chou Li Qing said something in Mandarin that made the chief grow pale.

"If these people are as dangerous as you say, why the order not to shoot?"

"The order comes from Beijing." The German smiled coldly. "Would you like to ask them why?"

The construction crews began arriving around half past seven, moving at a leisurely pace toward their assigned equipment. In short order, the dredges were powered up with a great roar of their diesel engines and the workday began in earnest. Sitting some 150 yards from the riverbank, the bucket-ladder dredge, looking almost toylike as its continuous conveyor of sharp-toothed buckets, stretching thirty feet into the air and fifty feet into the water, began scooping up endless loads of water, silt, and crushed rock to dump into a waiting barge tied alongside. Fifty yards away, a smaller drilling dredge began working its way through the bedrock at the water's edge while a suction dredge worked alongside. A string of barges was lined up waiting to be loaded with everything the dredges pulled up from the river bottom.

"We have police boats hidden on the other side of the river," the chief said, anticipating Max's question. "They cannot possibly get away."

Using a pair of binoculars, the three men scanned the incoming workers, hoping to catch a glimpse of the three fugitives. Minibuses would arrive, unload their passengers at the base of the new construction, and then depart only to return with another load of workers. There was a certain commonality in their appearance, similar clothes and safety helmets, yet he was looking for that small detail that would set them apart.

Some indication to show they were out of place, uncomfortable in these surroundings.

Finally, his efforts were rewarded. Max saw them moving with a group of workers along the road toward the barges at the base of the bridge scaffolding. Joe kept the boy between them as they walked on.

"I see them." Chou Li Qing moved his binoculars in an arch to take in more of the river activity. "There is a boat coming around the end barge."

"Chief, tell your people to move in now," Max said, as they watched their prey intently.

The crowd of workers seemed to thin out as each construction gang broke away from the group heading back to their individual jobs at the site. Finally, Max could see the three fugitives were alone as they walked down the narrow path where the scaffolding ended. Climbing a steep ladder, the trio boarded the nearest barge just as a line of uniformed police suddenly emerged from hiding and charged forward down the road behind them. At that instant, loud sirens began to blare as police boats surged forward from the opposite bank of the river.

JOE TOSSED THE HARD HATS AWAY AS THEY BEGAN RUNNING ALONG the walkway of the empty barge. When they reached the end, he grabbed Charley around the waist, and they jumped across the small open span to the next barge tied to the ladder-bucket dredge. The vessel shuddered with the continuous efforts of the buckets. Rushing to capture the suspects, the police quickly followed but they were slowed by the single-file narrow walkways.

SKIRTING THE PERIMETER OF THE BARGE, THE FUGITIVES MADE THEIR way to a small gangway and boarded the dredge. Max watched as they raced across the fantail and disappeared over the side of the dredge.

"Where are they?" Max screamed.

Moments later, a small speedboat shot into view, turning away from the construction. Three police boats gave chase, cutting off their escape upriver. The smaller boat turned sharply, reversed course, and tried to maneuver between the dredges and waiting barges at full speed. Two of the larger police boats broke off the pursuit, staying back to block any chance of escape across the river. The third persisted, eventually trapping the fugitives.

For a long moment, the two boats sat still in the water, facing one another. Max's palms began to sweat, his grip on the binoculars tightened as he watched the two warriors sizing up their opponents. Construction workers on the dredges and barges lined the railings to watch the chase. They could hear the police demanding the people on board the motor boat surrender, but they couldn't see any movement. With the second demand over the loudspeaker, the small boat suddenly lurched forward in the water, its engines at full power. The only possible avenue of escape was a narrow shaft of space between a barge loaded with debris and the hull of the bucket dredge. The speedboat shot through the opening just as the barge drifted toward the dredge, clipping the back transom of the speeding boat. It careened off the hull of the dredge, the helmsman desperately tried to regain control of the craft without losing power. First, he overcompensated in one direction and then in the other, sending the speeding vessel skidding along the hull of the big dredger. As the onlookers watched helplessly, it snagged an anchor cable as it neared the bow. In an instant, the speeding boat was caught in the swirling whirlpool created by the buckets clawing at the river bottom. As the huge buckets crashed into the small boat, the sound of splintering wood followed by the explosion of the gasoline tanks could be heard at the police command post on top of the warehouse a short distance away.

"What happened?" The chief was ashen-faced. The three men stood silently staring at the flaming carnage strewn across the water and up the bucket ladder.

"I want to see the bodies!" Max was grim. Slowly, he turned and walked away, leaving the chief to deal with the aftermath.

⁓

FOR A BRIEF MOMENT, THE SUDDEN IMPACT AND FIREBALL FROZE the crew of the dredger as they stood along the rail, mesmerized by the flaming debris falling on the bucket conveyor. It was only a momentary delay, and then orders were shouted and men began running, setting in motion a well-rehearsed routine for dealing with both collision and fire. By the time fire hoses were trained on the crash site, the remains of the speedboat had either sunk or were reduced to burning wreckage floating on the surface. Burning fuel, napalm-like, had reached the top of the bucket ladder by the time the fire hoses were turned in that direction. A lifeboat was launched to mix in with the police boats and other river traffic that had descended on the area to render assistance. To the casual observer, it would seem to be an incredibly chaotic scene, with little or no potential for positive results.

It took nearly five hours for the cleanup and recovery efforts at the site to be concluded. Search-and-rescue teams had recovered partial remains of three victims, but they were little more than body parts. The victims had been torn apart by the explosion and badly burned to the point of making identification impossible.

"What are you going to tell the Bai Lang?" Sitting behind his desk at police headquarters, the chief was visibly frightened. There was a slight tremor in his fingers as he lit a cigarette.

Max ignored the question, simply staring out the window. The continued silence was only broken by the incessant opening and closing of his Zippo lighter. The constant clicking, like a dripping faucet, was grating on the nerves.

"He is expecting us to call," Chou Li Qing urged.

"You call," the German finally said, getting to his feet and pocketing the lighter.

"I can't call him, Max!" Chou Li Qing almost whined. "The Bai Ling gave you the job of finding the boy. He trusted you, not me. What can I tell him?"

"The truth." Max, grim-faced, turned to look at them. In ten years he had never failed the Bai Lang. What would he do if the boy was dead? "We don't know what happened."

SEVENTEEN

THE EIGHTEEN-FOOT BOX TRUCK HAD AN EXTENDED CREW CAB that made the long drive to Xian at least bearable if not comfortable for the five passengers. Essentially, it was an uneventful trip. The drive from Yinchuan was long—a little less than seven hours—but all in all, they made good time. Avoiding the semicircular drive entrance of the Xian Sheraton Hotel, they parked at the curb out of the traffic lane. It was precisely four in the afternoon.

"Now what?" Yu Tang asked as he turned in the driver's seat so he could see the passengers in the back of the crew cab and still keep an eye on the cars pulling up to the hotel entrance.

"We wait for the Mandarin Tour buses to arrive," Ai Tian said.

The five passengers sat in silence for the next few minutes, each lost in his or her own thoughts, watching the comings and goings at the hotel entrance.

"Ai Tian." The concern in Joe's voice was clear. "How long before the German figures out what we did?"

"Oh, I imagine he already suspects." The businessman smiled. "The problem is he can't really report back to the Bai Lang until he knows for sure. And it will take the Yinchuan police two or three days to run the DNA tests on the bodies they found in the river."

"The whole thing gives me the creeps!" Charley stated softly.

"Don't worry, we didn't hurt anyone." Ai Tian tried to be reassuring. "I have a friend at the medical school. We borrowed some leftover parts from the pathology department."

"Somehow that makes it worse!" Charley seemed to pull himself back into the seat.

"The whole thing was Tony's idea." Ai Tian said it with a good deal of pride. "He built the remote-controlled speedboat for a film that was supposed to start shooting next week. I guess they will have to wait for him to build a new one."

"The buses are here." Yu Tang got out of the truck and walked around to the passenger side to open the doors. They huddled together on the sidewalk beside the truck until Vicki finally spoke up.

"I don't know how to thank you both for everything you have done for us."

"I am happy that we could help," Yu Tang said, shaking hands with Joe and Charley.

"I think my great-grandfather would be very proud." Ai Tian embraced each of them in turn. He said something to Charley in Mandarin that made the boy smile.

"What will you do now?" Joe asked.

"Carry on with my business, of course." His smile carried a mischievous glint before turning serious. "I have a truckload of uniforms to deliver to the chief of police here in Xian. And then there is the matter of the death of a prisoner in the Yinchuan police headquarters that I would like to discuss with him." His expression was tinged with a little sadness. "There is much to do."

"We have to go." Joe led them along the pathway, crossing the drive toward the wide glass door entrance, they joined the weary Mandarin Tour passengers disembarking from the buses.

The two-story-high oval rotunda lobby was dominated by an enormous crystal chandelier. The lobby was paved in black granite with a multicolored granite mosaic compass rose centered below the chandelier. A pair of wide stairways curved downward from the mezzanine to the lobby forming large, squared archways on either side.

Once inside, the trio stopped in the center of the lobby briefly getting their bearings. In another moment they were surrounded by the other Mandarin Tour passengers. An archway on the right led to the reception desk and the elevators to the upper floors, while the bell desk was tucked away on the left.

"Over there." Joe indicated a large table bearing the Mandarin Tour Company banner set up near the staircase on the left. Their favorite tour guide was passing out room keys.

"Ah, the Thomas family, you are in room 1804." Gail Warren sorted through the stack of envelopes and handed Joe the room key cards, smiling, and then spoke softly. "Your luggage has been put in the room, courtesy of Mr. Fitzpatrick. Are you guys okay?"

"We're fine, thanks, Gail," Joe replied.

As they moved off toward the elevators with several other tour members, Gail raised her voice to make a general announcement.

"Remember, everyone: breakfast starts at seven thirty, and then we are back on the buses at nine thirty. We have a full schedule for tomorrow, so don't be late."

Room 1804 was actually a minisuite at the end of the hall on the eighteenth floor. The view of the city was excellent. It was one large bedroom and sitting area consisting of two queen-size beds, two night tables, and an L-shaped desk in the corner near the window. A low dresser with three sets of drawers and a minibar covered one wall. A disproportionately wide flat-screen TV was mounted above the dresser.

"I want to take a hot bath," Vicki said with a deep sigh and stretched out on the bed nearest the window.

Joe dropped the backpack on the first bed and pulled out his scanner. Without a word, he began checking the room for any sign of a hidden microphone or camera. Finding nothing, he returned the small electronic device to the backpack.

"What do we do now?" Charley asked. The boy had waited for Joe to finish scanning before speaking. He spoke quietly, seemingly drained of energy.

"We stick to our original plan." Joe checked the closet and pulled out their luggage. "And we get cleaned up, pick out a change of clothes, and get a good night's sleep."

Maintaining the image of a vacationing family, Joe had ordered an American-style dinner. Unfortunately, the three fugitives didn't have too much of an appetite. By eight thirty, Joe pushed the room service cart out into the hall. After securely locking the door, he came back into the room and pulled the drapes closed. Dropping down on the couch, Joe stretched his legs across the coffee table and let the tension ease out of his body.

"Shall we find out what's happening in the world?" He turned the television to CNN.

"Beijing police have reported that an American tourist witnessed an attempted purse snatching on the Great Wall this afternoon," the CNN reporter stated. "It seems some local Chinese merchants foiled the would-be criminal and held him for police." The reporter looked up from his script and continued. "Police Inspector Chou Kong-Sang of the Beijing Municipal Security Service would like the American tourist who witnessed the attempted mugging to contact his office as soon as possible."

"Why would they lie like that?" Vicki asked.

"They don't want to create a panic during the height of the tourist season," Joe replied. "Normally, CNN would never have run this story—it just isn't that important. But I think Inspector Chou wanted to send us a message, and this was the only way he could do it."

"Do you think he knew we were going to be on the wall?" Charley asked.

"No." Joe shook his head. "If Inspector Chou knew we were going to be there, he would have had five hundred cops waiting for us." He turned off the television and, after a moment, reached for his laptop. "The thing that keeps nagging at me is how the hell did the bad guys know we were going to be there?"

As he placed the small computer on the coffee table, raised the screen, and pressed the power button, Charley suddenly leaped off the bed, yelling.

"No!" The boy yanked it away, slammed the cover down to shut off the power, and ejected the battery.

"Charley!" Vicki shouted. "What are you doing?"

"I just remembered that Joe checked his emails at the hotel the night before we went to the Great Wall." He looked from one confused face to the other. "This computer was the only outside contact we had. It's the only way they could have known that we were going to the wall. Do you have a small screwdriver?"

Joe handed over the Swiss Army knife. Using the Phillips-head screwdriver, Charley removed the back panel from the laptop.

"They didn't know where we were going to be, only that we were with one of the Mandarin Tour groups," Joe said, "Terri was right."

"And this is how they knew." Charley pointed to a small cylinder, about an inch long, wedged into the guts of the computer. "This doesn't belong in your laptop. It probably sends out a GPS signal or something when you turn on the power." He pulled the cylinder free of its connections and dropped it on the coffee table.

"Once they knew which hotel, all they had to do was start checking the guests."

"I think Mandarin was the only tour company at the hotel," Vicki added.

Joe stared at the little cylinder for a long moment before reaching across the table and placing it in a stone candy dish. Using the butt of the Swiss Army knife and the stone dish like a mortar and pestle, he ground the little electronic spy into a powder.

THE BAI LANG SAT IN SEMIDARKNESS, STARING OUT THE WINDOW at the late-night Beijing skyline. He loved the view from the penthouse. On any other night, the sight would be relaxing, even soothing, but not tonight. He listened intently as Max and Chou Li Qing recounted the events of that morning.

"What do we know for certain?" he finally asked.

Max was slow to reply, thinking over his answer with care. The Bai Lang watched him toy with an antique bronze dagger that was sitting on the coffee table.

"I think they escaped," Max said, facing his boss.

"What about the bodies?"

"Because of the explosion and fire, we only have body parts." Chou Li Qing commented. "But the DNA tests will take another day or two."

"Why do you think they escaped?"

"Because it was too neat, almost as if it was planned—well planned," Max said.

"If you are correct, then we have other questions to answer. Who helped them? How did they do it? And, most importantly, where are they now?"

Chou Li Qing said something in Mandarin.

"I understand." The Bai Lang looked away from the two men and contemplated the view for several minutes. "How did you know they would be on the wall?"

"Sun Wang Ji managed to install a GPS transponder in the American's computer," Chou Li Qing stated. "But it only works if he turns on the laptop."

"Sun Wang Ji guessed that they were with one of the tour groups going to the wall." Max explained.

"What are you saying? Could they be hiding with a tour group now?"

"It's possible," Max responded. "The problem is we don't know where to start looking."

"I think we must start thinking like tourists," Chou Li Qing said quietly. "It will be easier for the American to blend in where there are a great many American tourists around him."

"So we need to look at our country's tourist attractions." The Bai Lang reached for the cordless phone on the table beside him. "I must make some calls. It's time for us to get some help."

EiGHTEEN

THE SKIES HAD BEGUN TURNING FROM DARK TO GRAY WHEN JOE opened his eyes. Although the couch was comfortable enough, he had not slept well or too soundly—but he had slept. The problem was that his mind, even his subconscious, kept returning to the unanswered questions that were eating away at him.

What will they do with Charley if they take him? So far, they seem to want him alive—they need him alive! We just have to stay ahead of them until Friday—then we're safe.

He stayed on the couch as the gray gave way and the room slowly filled with weak morning light. Pushing himself upright against the pillows, Joe looked over at his two roommates sleeping peacefully. The covers slid halfway down as Vicki turned on her side toward the window. The curtains allowed just enough sunlight through to frame her face with a soft, almost angelic glow. It reminded Joe of an Italian Renaissance painting he'd seen somewhere. He smiled at the thought.

On the other hand, Charley had slipped between the two large pillows on the second bed and fallen asleep with his jade dragon clutched tightly in his hand the minute he crawled into bed. At some point during the night he must have been dreaming because Joe heard him moaning softly.

Finally, when he couldn't procrastinate any longer, Joe pulled himself off the couch and headed for the shower. The movement was greeted with sore muscles and stiffness. He needed a good workout, but that would have to wait a few more days.

Their suitcases were packed, tagged and in the hall by seven thirty, in accordance with the Mandarin Tours instruction sheet left in the room. Joe repacked the backpack and checked the small package yet again. Tucking the semiautomatic pistol into the waistband at the small of his back, Joe led the way down the hall to the elevators.

"I don't know about the two of you, but I'm hungry." He winked at Charley as he pressed the button for the mezzanine.

The banquet room entrance was draped with Mandarin Tours banners and flanked by photo posters of guided side trips along the tour route. A small table staffed by two hotel staff members was being used as a check-in desk for tour members.

"It's open seating, Mr. Thomas." The young clerk checked their names off the list. "Enjoy your breakfast."

AT NINE THIRTY PRECISELY, GAIL ANNOUNCED THAT IT WAS TIME to board the buses and get the day underway. Joining the stream of Mandarin Tours sightseers heading down the twin curved stairways to the hotel lobby and out to the buses, they followed Gail to bus number one. As they stood in line to board, Gail gave them quick, quiet instructions.

"Take the seat directly behind the driver. Charley, you sit with me in the front row on the right."

"Tell me again why we're still on this tour?" Vicki asked as they took their seats.

"Fitzpatrick won't be ready until tomorrow afternoon. The Bai Lang isn't sure if we survived yesterday's explosion or not. So, at least this way, we have some protection, and we can see them coming." Joe tried to exude more confidence than he felt.

One more day, he thought. *One more day on the run, and then we get to Shanghai and we're home free.*

Fifteen minutes later, the caravan of Mandarin Tours yellow coaches began working its way through traffic. The hour long drive would take them along Feng Hao Road until it became Xignan Straight Street. Turning left onto Huanshery West Road, they would eventually pick up the S311 Expressway on their way to the Lishan Garden.

"Good morning, again." As usual, Gail Warren was bright and enthusiastic in her presentation. Holding several brochures in one hand and the microphone in the other, she continued her introduction to the schedule of events. "We are on our way to the mausoleum park of the first emperor of unified China. Commonly referred to as Lishan Garden, the park is about 558 acres and contains the tomb of Emperor Qin Shi Huang!" As with most of her tour groups, there was nothing to indicate any recognition of the name. After a moment, she continued. "He is the emperor who built the Great Wall and created the Terracotta Army that we will see this morning." Now, there was a murmur of acknowledgement.

"Charley, you are his direct descendant," Vicki whispered. "And the descendants of the Imperial Guard, the Terracotta Army, are the people helping us stay alive."

A moment later, Charley picked up a stack of brochures from Gail's bag and walked down the aisle passing them out as she spoke. Joe touched Vicki's arm to draw her attention to the boy. Gail smiled and continued with her presentation.

"Okay, some reminders, there will be lots of tours at the museum today, so make sure you get back on the right bus." She watched their reactions carefully. Losing a tourist at the Terracotta Warriors Museum was not a good career move.

"We are group number one," Gail announced, waving a small, yellow pennant emblazoned with a green number. Someone in the back of the bus cheered.

"I like your enthusiasm." She moved back and forth along the aisle as she spoke into the microphone. "Now, once we get inside the park, it's a little bit of a walk through the gardens to pit number one, so keep an eye out for my flag so you don't get separated from our group."

"What's a pit number one?" the tourist with the long-lensed Nikon asked.

"Pit number one is the largest of the four sites and contains thousands of life-size terracotta warriors, horses, bronze chariots and all kinds of weapons." Gail went on to describe the four primary excavation sites, explaining how they were continuing to discover new artifacts on a daily basis.

"We are very lucky to have Dr. Chen Xiao guiding us through the museum today. He is the leading archaeologist working on the terracotta warriors project and the head of the archaeological team from Oxford University."

Morning traffic wasn't too heavy as a result the caravan made good time arriving at the parking area in just under an hour. The four Mandarin buses were directed to parking spaces near the main entrance. The driver shut down the engine, opened the door and stepped out to assist the thirty-two passengers down the steps. Gail motioned Vicki and Joe to stay in their seats until everyone else had disembarked. When the last passenger had passed them, she leaned across the aisle and whispered to Joe.

"Leave the gun pushed down between the seats. They have metal detectors at the entrance to the park, and we don't need to set off any alarms."

They followed Gail's yellow pennant across the parking area to the entrance of the park. Despite the early hour, the park was hosting a considerable crowd of sightseers, some already inside, and some waiting to be admitted. Tour groups use a separate entrance off to one side and, thanks to the close proximity of their parking space, Mandarin Tours group one was the first through the turnstiles.

From the main entrance, it was a pleasant fifteen-minute walk through the gardens beneath a bright, clear sky that held the promise of a warm, comfortable day. They followed the path as it worked its way over gentle hills, probably man-made, and through a thin forest of trees until finally opening onto a large plaza surrounded by a number of oversized buildings.

For the most part, they had walked in silence, enjoying their surroundings. The group had gotten spread out somewhat, a great ellipse of people, fast walkers and stragglers, following Gail and her pennant toward the largest of the buildings on the far side of the plaza.

"I was wondering," Joe asked, "what are your plans once we get to Los Angeles?"

"I don't really know." Vicki seemed stunned by the question. "I've been too busy and too frightened to think beyond getting Charley out of the country. I guess Mr. Fitzpatrick has some ideas."

"Don't rely on the federal government to take care of you. You'd get lost in the bureaucracy." He was thoughtful for a moment. "I'll talk to him when we get to Shanghai."

"Thank you."

"Of course, you know, you could stay with me." He said it almost as an aside. "I have a big house with plenty of room. There's only me, the housekeeper, and the cook. Eva would be very happy to have someone to cook for again. Besides, you have to get Charley into a good school."

"That is very kind of you, but you have done so much for us already—you are doing so much." She turned to face him, a wave of emotion evident in her eyes. "Are you sure you want more of us?"

"It's not a problem." Joe smiled reassuringly. "Just think about it, and we can talk to Fitzpatrick about the idea when we get to Shanghai. Besides, I'm just getting used to the pleasure of your company."

"Me too." Vicki took his hand in hers as they continued walking across the plaza.

As the tour group gathered around their guide, Joe realized that they were standing in an open plaza fully exposed. The irony was that they were just another group of tourists among dozens of groups. He still kept scanning the area, hoping not to spot a threat that he knew would come eventually.

Gail stopped near the entrance of the largest building in the complex and spoke with a Chinese gentleman who seemed to be waiting for her. Afterward, she held her pennant up high and waited for the stragglers to catch up. When her group was finally gathered around, she introduced her companion. Dr. Chen Xiao was in his midfifties, lean, fit, well dressed, and nearly matching Gail in height.

"Good morning, I am to be your guide on your trip back into the very early years of China's history." He began to lead the group up the steps toward the entrance of the building. "Everything that you will see today is just a small fraction of the mausoleum complex designed for Emperor Qin Shi Huang. He was the first leader to unify the warring states of China."

"What year was all of this built?" one of the group asked.

"Construction of the tomb and the terracotta warriors was begun in 246 BCE when the emperor first ascended the throne. That's about two thousand five hundred years ago. The emperor was thirteen at the time."

"How long did the construction take?" Charley asked.

"It took about forty years and seven hundred thousand workers to complete the work, including the warriors." The group followed him through the double doors of the building. They stood at the railing of the thirty-foot-wide walkway that wound around the perimeter of the building and overlooked the excavation twenty feet below.

"This building is known as Vault One or Pit One. It is the largest of the excavations," Dr. Xiao explained. "You are looking at the vanguard of the Terracotta Army placed here to protect the emperor in the afterlife."

The building itself was almost as impressive as the pit. As large as a professional football stadium, it covered an excavation measuring more than 750 feet long by 203 feet wide and containing more than six thousand figures. He went on to explain that there are eleven brick-paved corridors ten feet wide separating the ranks of armed soldiers. The warriors were set in place as if ready for a battle, with ranks of archers and war chariots for tactical support. They were facing east, toward the source of greatest threat to Emperor Qin Shi Huang at the time.

"Each of these figures is unique, presumably modeled after the original members of the Imperial Guard." Dr. Xiao began leading the group along the perimeter railing as he explained the history of the warriors.

"How many terracotta warriors are buried in the tomb?" Someone asked.

"Good question." Dr. Xiao smiled. "We don't really know for sure, but the estimates are somewhere around eight to ten thousand warriors. But that doesn't count the horses, war chariots, and imperial chariots that have been discovered."

As he led the group along the observation walkway, Dr. Xiao described the methods used in creating the terracotta warriors, their weapons, armor, horses, and chariots as well as the painstaking process of recovering and restoring the figures from their centuries of burial.

"Why are they all the same color?" an older woman in the Mandarin group asked.

"Does anyone know why?" Dr. Xiao commented.

"I mean, if they are supposed to be lifelike, you would think they would have painted them to look like people," she continued.

"Actually, they did." Dr. Xiao stopped and stood at the railing. It had taken more than an hour to circumnavigate the excavation. "Do you see the two figures in this first section?" He pointed to the kneeling archers some twenty-five feet from their vantage point. "You can just see some faint discoloration along the sides and chests of the warriors. Originally, they were beautifully painted with brilliant polychrome colors. The problem with being twenty-five hundred years old is that the paint oxidized within seconds of being exposed to the air and just flaked off."

The group stood for a long moment watching three technicians working in the pit. The level of difficulty involved in removing centuries of debris from the delicate figures became very evident.

"The new exhibition hall has displays of replicas of the terracotta warriors with their original polychrome painting."

Dr. Xiao led the group out the way they had come. At the bottom of the steps he moved off to the left and waited for stragglers to catch up. Gail made a quick head count and indicated everyone was present.

"All right, now we have a choice to make." Dr. Xiao smiled at his audience. "We can continue on to Pits Two and Three or go directly to the new exhibition."

"So, tell me something," the Nikon tourist said. "Do these other pits have terracotta warriors in 'em?"

"Yes."

"And do they have terracotta horses and a bronze chariot or two?"

"Yes."

"Then, I guess we've seen 'em already." A chorus of laughter ran through the group. "What's in the new exhibition hall?"

The group followed Dr. Xiao and Gail's yellow pennant across the plaza to the new Emperor Qin Shi Huang Museum Exhibition Pavilion. It was a huge bow-truss-roofed building with high ceilings, slightly larger than the structure protecting Pit One. Once inside the foyer, the differences in exhibition style were remarkable. It was a dark, massive hall with sparse overhead lights spaced few and far between. Theatrical spotlights and floodlights throughout the hall were focused on the individual exhibits and showcases leaving the rest of the room in a relative semigloom. Not quite dark but not bright light either.

"The purpose of this series of displays is to give you an idea of what it was like to be here twenty-five centuries ago as the tomb was being built." He led them to the first very large glass-enclosed display to the right of the entrance. The display was about two feet below floor level to give the viewer an overview of the setting.

"This is a recreation of General Tzu's field headquarters the way it would have looked in the second century BC," Dr. Xiao explained.

Five figures representing the general and his staff officers, dressed in the colorful uniforms of the Imperial Guard, were standing around a fair-sized wooden table that sat on a small hill. The table was littered with maps, drawings, and various items of daily life from two thousand years ago. A tent, presumably the general's quarters, was set up a little beyond the table. A half dozen archers and infantry men were positioned around the perimeter to protect their commander. Everything in the display, from the uniforms to the tent, cooking utensils, and a small bronze bell on the table, bore the image of the imperial dragon.

"General Sun Tzu was the commanding officer of the Imperial Guard and supervised the construction of the emperor's tomb."

"How did they make the warriors?" someone in the group asked. "Were they made here or brought from somewhere else?"

"Actually, it's fascinating that they came up with this idea twenty-five centuries ago." Dr. Xiao smiled. "They were made in kind of an assembly-line operation with the head and facial features being the final elements. Some say that each figure was modeled after a member of the Imperial Guard. But who knows?"

"Excuse me, Dr. Xiao," Joe said. "I keep seeing this dragon image everywhere. Is this the same dragon that we saw in the Forbidden City?"

"It is the same," Dr. Xiao stated. "Dragons are sacred in Chinese history and mythology dating back some three thousand years. You will see dragons all over, even in modern China, but only the imperial family is permitted to use the image of a dragon with five claws." He began walking toward the next exhibit as he spoke.

"The image of the five-clawed dragon represents the emperor and his direct connection to heaven." Dr. Xiao explained as they continued moving down the aisle. "General Tzu has written that the dragon is the power of the emperor but the Dragon's Claw enforces and safeguards that power. And, of course, he nicknamed the Imperial Guard the Dragon's Claw!"

"See, Charley," Vicki spoke softly, "even after twenty-five hundred years the Dragon's Claw is still protecting the emperor."

The aisles between exhibits were becoming increasingly congested as more people filled the hall. It wasn't really crowded yet, but in another hour or two, it promised to become a mob scene. A number of tour groups were working their ways through the exhibits from entrances at either end of the huge building. Despite tour guides and museum employee's best efforts, the noise level had become a constant backdrop—not loud enough to be disturbing but always present.

Dr. Xiao stood beside a large glass-enclosed case sitting on a platform that rose some twelve inches above the floor. The overhead spotlights gave the bronze sculpture an iridescent quality that shimmered in the artificial light. He motioned the group to come in closer.

"This horse-drawn chariot and driver was one of the earliest discoveries at this site."

"Yeah, but they can't be life-size like the warriors?" one of the tourists observed.

"No, you're right," Dr. Xiao replied. "The horses, driver, and chariot are actually half-sized. This war chariot and the enclosed imperial chariot across the aisle are made of bronze and inlaid with pure gold and silver."

"That's why it glitters!" Mr. Nikon had a keen eye.

"We know from General Tzu's writings that these were modeled after the chariots actually used by Emperor Qin Shi Huang to inspect the troops or check the progress of construction of the tomb."

As they continued along the line of restored figures, moving from one display to the next, Joe tried to listen to the lecture as they walked. But the growing crowd surrounding them was becoming a distraction. Keeping Charley between himself and Vicki, he stayed as close to Dr. Xiao as possible.

Near the center of the museum, they approached a large display of restored and painted terracotta warriors showing various types of weapons typically carried by the Imperial Guard. Dr. Xiao stepped up on a raised platform and called their attention to an assortment of swords, axes, spears, daggers, and crossbows laid out on a small table.

"These are just a few of the weapons carried by the Imperial Guard as they went into battle." He held up a three-foot-long blade. "This is a bronze *jian*—a sword in Chinese. It was found in the first pit we saw today."

"It looks brand-new!" someone commented from the back of the group.

"With the exception of the handle, this is exactly what it looked like when it was found." Dr. Xiao held up the blade in one hand and passed a single sheet of white paper to one of the tourists gathered before him. "Can you hold this between your hands?"

"Sure." The tourist from the Bell Tower held the paper firmly.

After a moment, with a little bit of dramatic fanfare, Dr. Xiao slowly and gently drew the *jian* across the taut sheet of paper, slicing it cleanly in half. "This sword is razor sharp and over two thousand years old!"

"How come it's still so sharp and shiny?" someone else asked.

"The metallurgy of the Qin dynasty, that's 221 BC to 206 BC, was far ahead of Western Europe." Joe noticed that Dr. Xiao watched his audience, enjoying playing off their astonishment. "They were using chromium in alloys centuries before the West knew what to do with it. All these weapons were far in advance of anything being made in England and France at that time."

"What's that funny-looking crossbow?" the Nikon tourist asked.

"Ah, you are going to love this one. Did you know that the crossbow was invented in China?" Dr. Xiao picked up a bow with a rectangular box built into the top of the stock. "This particular bow has a modern-day descendant called a machine gun."

Mr. Nikon was dubious. "You're kidding, right?"

"No, I'm serious." He opened the box and held it up in one hand while displaying an arrow in the other. "An archer could load fifteen to eighteen bolts or arrows like this one into this box. He could then rapid fire one bolt after another by simply cocking the bow. An archer could even fire two arrows at a time." Dr. Xiao replaced the ancient weapon on the table. "And they were amazingly accurate."

Joe froze, his eyes drawn to the far end of the hall. Raised voices. Shouts. A line of uniformed officers and men in dark suits were moving into the hall, blocking the exits.

Dr. Xiao's hand reached for the crossbow on the table, his gaze searching the crowd. The men were not police. And the men in suits were asking people for ID. Then he saw their leader.

A SUDDEN RUSH OF RAISED VOICES AT THE FAR END OF THE HALL drew their attention. From his vantage point on the raised platform, Dr. Xiao could see a line of uniformed officers moving into the hall and blocking the exits at both ends of the building. They weren't police. He recognized the Ministry of Justice security uniforms. There were several men wearing dark suits directing the officers as they began methodically moving through the crowd. They seemed to be asking for identification. At that moment, he saw and instantly recognized the man commanding the search.

QUICKLY LEANING DOWN, HE TOUCHED VICKI'S ARM AND WHISPERED something in Chinese. Pointing toward the right side of the exhibition hall, he urged her to move quickly.

Joe was already pivoting, his hand on Charley's shoulder.

"We have to leave right now!" Vicki took Charley's other arm as she spoke.

"What's going on?" Joe asked. "What is this guy telling you?"

"Dr. Xiao is a friend!" The urgency in Vicki's voice was clear.

"Wei Yung-Cheng and his thugs are searching the crowd for you," Dr. Xiao replied, stepping off the platform. "You must get out of here fast!"

"Why? He's the deputy minister of justice. I met him in Beijing."

"He is the Bai Lang—the leader of the Bai Lang tong that is hunting for you." He pointed Joe toward the small, unmarked staff door on the right side of the pavilion. "Go through that door and then down the hall to the exit on the right. I will meet you in the staff parking lot." He stepped back up on the platform to check the progress of the security teams.

"Move quickly but don't run." Joe herded Vicki and Charley through the thickening crowd amid a rising noise level. People were getting nervous and moving away from the continuing security search at the far end of the room.

Bai Lang. The White Wolf. Wendy's words came screaming back to Joe. The leader of one of the oldest criminal gangs in China, like your Mafia only better organized. No wonder they were ahead of us at every step.

They had gone little more than thirty yards through the crowd when Joe was suddenly seized from behind by two men. With a burly uniformed officer on each side trying to secure his arms, Joe was momentarily immobilized. He glanced up just as a third man grabbed Vicki and Charley tightly by the wrists.

"Joe!" Vicki screamed.

The man was huge, looking more like a sumo wrestler than a security guard, he held a captive tightly in each hand and began yelling triumphantly. His victory was short-lived. In that split second, a bronze-tipped arrow fired from an ancient crossbow sliced through his shirt, shattered three ribs, perforated his aorta, and shredded his heart. Ashen-faced, he stood still for a moment, the grip on his captives slackening, before falling to the floor.

Instantly, Joe extended his arms around the backs of his attackers and then pulled his arms forward and together with all the strength built up from a lifetime of weight lifting, almost as if he were playing a giant pair of cymbals. Their heads collided with a dull, sickening sound. One dropped to the floor unconscious while the other struggled to reach a pistol on his belt. A quick fist to the jaw ended his efforts.

Looking back, he saw Dr. Xiao waving them on toward the side door. As Vicki and Charley rushed to his side, Joe took the pistol from their attacker. Taking careful aim, Joe fired three shots harmlessly into the solid wooden base of the nearest display. The sound of the gunshots echoed and was magnified in the cavernous exhibition hall. Instant panic spread through the crowd of tourists, visiting students, and security personnel alike, giving Joe the cover they needed. He didn't know for sure, maybe it was Confucius or General Tzu who'd said, "In chaos, there is opportunity." But now, at this moment, it meant escape.

Pulling Charley and Vicki in his wake, Joe shoved their way through the mass of frightened, panic-driven people. Once through the side door, they found a round vestibule with corridors that branched off in three directions.

"Now what?" Joe muttered. "Dr. Xiao said to go to the right."

"No!" Vicki said. "He said down the hall and the exit on the right."

"There's a directory behind you." Charley pointed out. "We need to go straight ahead."

"How do you know?" Joe asked.

"Because I can read Chinese!" Charley smirked. "This way."

"Smart-ass!" Joe muttered with a smile as they followed the boy down the hall.

NiNETEEN

"YOUR SITUATION HAS CHANGED," DR. XIAO CAUTIONED AS THEY followed him through a maze of bicycles, scooters, motorcycles, and cars parked haphazardly in the staff lot.

"Wei Yung-Cheng has come after you personally and openly. He will continue to hunt for you. And he will use the police or even the army."

Dr. Xiao stopped beside a big, powerful-looking motorcycle fitted with a sidecar.

"Can you drive a motorcycle?" he asked.

"It's been a while, but I can handle it," Joe said, accepting the offered key with thanks.

"I know that you must be in Shanghai tomorrow afternoon." He opened a small road map and spread it across the motorcycle seat. "Stay off the toll roads. Use the city streets and rural highways instead," Dr. Xiao instructed. "It is a little more than seven hundred miles, so if you have a little luck, it should take you about fifteen hours."

"I think we'll need more than a little luck." Joe studied the map carefully.

"The route is marked for you," he explained. "There is a small farming village about half way to Shanghai. We have friends in the village who will give you food and a safe place to sleep. I have written their contact information on the back of the map."

"What happens to you if they catch us with your motorcycle?" Joe asked.

"I will report it stolen the day after tomorrow." He smiled at the three fugitives. "So, don't get caught!"

"Why are you helping us?" Charley spoke softly, fixing his eyes on their benefactor, almost afraid of the answer.

"There may no longer be an empire," Dr. Xiao replied, as he rolled up his right shirt sleeve to reveal a small imperial dragon tattoo on the inside of his forearm. "But the Dragon's Claw will always protect the emperor." He bowed respectfully to the Son of Heaven.

"Thank you." Charley stood up ramrod straight and returned the gesture of respect.

WHEN THE SOUND OF GUN SHOTS REVERBERATED THROUGH THE cavernous museum, it created the desired panic among the tourists as well as the security forces. Wei Yung-Cheng pushed his way through the people crowding to get out the exit. He found a chair reserved for one of the museum staff and climbed up to get a better view.

"What the hell is going on?" He screamed into the two-way radio in Chinese. "Who fired those shots?"

The two-way radio crackled with static as multiple responders tried to broadcast as the same time. Finally, the security force captain got through to the deputy minister.

"We don't know where they came from!" There was another squelch of static. "I don't think it was any of my men."

"Get your men into the crowd and restore some order." Wei Yung-Cheng instinctively knew who had fired the shots. At least Max had chosen the right tour company. "I don't want a stampede of tourists trampling each other in a panic."

The crowd seemed to calm a little in the absence of further violence. Two or three minutes of radio silence was either reassuring or the calm before the storm.

"We have one dead and two unconscious!" The storm was Max speaking English on the radio. "We are just about in the middle of the room; you need to get your Ministry of Justice people here before someone calls the local police to report a murder!"

It took another hour to get the body removed, calm down the museum officials and the local police. Eventually, they were able to get the tourists moving out of the building with the promise of private tours behind the scenes at the excavations.

"Who is this Joe Wilder?" For Wei Yung-Cheng, it was a rhetorical question he really couldn't answer.

"I don't think he killed your man," the German commented. "He had to have help."

"Why do you say that?" Chou Li Chiang asked.

"The two men he knocked out didn't see who fired the arrow," Max replied. "It came from behind them and a little distance away. Every time we had him—on the wall, in the village, and Yinchuan—someone has helped him."

"So the question remains: Who is helping our little emperor?" the Bai Lang said, thoughtfully. "And why?"

"When you met Wilder at the embassy party, you said he was friendly with the American trade delegate?"

"Yes, but he was friendly with the ambassador, the congressman, and most of the businessmen who were at the party."

"I know, but could that trade delegate be helping Wilder?"

"Fitzpatrick? It is possible, I suppose."

"Perhaps I should have some of our people keep an eye on this man?" Chou Li Qing suggested. "Maybe I'll do it myself."

"And perhaps Max is right and Mr. Fitzpatrick is more than he seems," the deputy minister of justice said. "I will check with our intelligence people and see if they know him."

LEAVING THE LISHAN GARDENS, JOE STAYED CLOSE TO THE ROUTE their tour bus had taken earlier. He kept clear of the expressway and toll roads, choosing instead to join the flow of commuters moving toward the center of the city. Wearing their crash helmets, they looked like so many other young Chinese families on the road that morning and soon melted into the chaos of the late morning rush. As they skirted the old walled city of Xian, Joe soon learned that traffic lanes and rights of way didn't seem to exist on Chinese city streets. While the center line dividing one direction from another and red stoplights were more or less observed, everything else appeared to be at the whim of the individual driver.

Traffic in the suburbs seemed to worsen as Joe worked their way past the more modern neighborhoods of the city. The streets were wider here, lined with modern office buildings, apartments, and shops of every description.

Change the language on the signs, Joe thought, *and this could be any major city in any country in the world.*

An hour into their escape and no sign they were being followed. No sign of the police.

TWENTY

According to Dr. Xiao's map, the next intersection should lead to the expressway and the road to Shanghai. A massive steel-and-stone sculpture formed the centerpiece of a circular intersection. Five boulevards converged on the roundabout like the spokes of a wheel. Joe slowed the big motorcycle, downshifting and pulling near the side, uncertain of which road to take.

"There!" Vicki grabbed his arm. "It's the second street on the right."

Signs in English and Chinese pointed the way to the G-40 Hushan Expressway.

"We have to stay off the toll roads if we can!" Joe shouted over the roar of the motorcycle engine and the surrounding traffic. It was difficult for Vicki to study the map with Charley sitting in her lap in the sidecar.

"Stay on the G-40 toll road for the next ten miles. We can get off before the toll booth. After that, we can take the Sheng Dao Provincial Road. It's slower but should be safer."

Joe nodded and then checked his watch. Barely three and a half hours had elapsed since they'd boarded that damn tour bus. He hoped traffic would thin out as they made their way out of the suburbs and into less populated territory.

Another ten minutes and Joe slowed the powerful bike to exit the toll road. Turning east, they crossed the Bahe River and joined the stream of vehicles on the rural highway.

"Why aren't we going faster?" Charley shouted, pointing out the gaps in traffic.

"If we just keep up with the other cars and trucks," Joe explained, "there will be no reason for the police to notice us."

The suburbs soon gave way to large areas of farm land interspersed with an occasional village. Once in a while, they passed an industrial park surrounded by a small town, newly built to support the factories.

Thirty minutes later, Joe maneuvered the motorcycle back onto the Provincial Road beyond the toll booths. It was another ten miles, according to the map, before they made the transition to the G-70 Expressway. By that time, traffic had thinned out considerably and he was able to increase speed to make better time.

"The turn off to Dr. Xiao's village will be about two hours past the Qinling Tunnel," Joe said. "It will be better if we can get there before dark."

The Qinling Tunnel was an eighteen-kilometer-long engineering marvel cut through the heart of the Qinling Mountain range that separated the Lintong District of Xian from China's eastern coastal plain. As they neared the entrance, the four-lane road narrowed down to two, slowing traffic to a crawl until they were barely moving more than three or four miles an hour.

"What's the matter?" Vicki asked.

"I don't know." Joe looked around, half expecting to find a police roadblock ahead, but found nothing alarming.

"Can I see?" Charley climbed out of the sidecar to straddle the motorcycle in front of Joe. "I read about this tunnel. They planted all kinds of trees inside and painted the roof to look like a blue sky with white clouds."

"Why would they do that?" Vicki asked.

"At first, it was just so long and the inside looked the same for mile after mile that drivers would fall asleep. What's the word in English?" He didn't wait for an answer. "Oh yeah, it was monotonous! So they did the trees and roof to keep people awake."

Once the two lanes of traffic moved through the massive opening in the mountain, they were greeted by banana palms, tropical ferns, and various types of greenery planted along the roadside. The clouds in the bright blue summer sky painted on the roof seemed to fade, and drivers once again focused on reaching their destination. Within ten minutes, the big bike was back up to sixty miles an hour.

The downslope run from the Qinling Tunnel to the fertile coastal plain was relatively uneventful. The long stretches of farmland with a few villages and an occasional town scattered among the miles of green crops were a pleasant contrast to the rock-strewn mountains they had just crossed.

Occasionally, the expressway dwindled down to a two-lane rural road as it passed through or around a town. As the sun inched down on the horizon, there were fewer and fewer vehicles on the road. By six o'clock, the sun had disappeared entirely and dusk was beginning to turn into darkness. Joe began to wonder if they had enough gasoline to reach Shanghai.

"Do you know where we turn off for the village?" He shouted over the engine noise.

"It should be the next road to the right." Vicki yelled back.

TWENTY-ONE

DR. XIAO'S VILLAGE WAS SIMPLY A CLUSTER OF FIFTEEN OR TWENTY buildings at the end of a narrow mostly unpaved track. The small town square was surrounded by three of the bigger buildings in the village. An ancient Taoist temple was the largest of these with a combination general store and party meeting hall on the right. The building on the left appeared to be a family residence but seemed much larger than the others. The remainder of the buildings seemed to be homes of various sizes and ages. All in all, Joe guessed the village housed some five or six hundred people.

It seemed eerily deserted as they drove slowly along the narrow road. Approaching the square, they saw a lone figure standing beside the entrance to the party meeting hall. Smiling, he waved a greeting and motioned them to stop. When Joe parked the bike in front of the hall, Vicki climbed out of the sidecar and approached the man cautiously. Joe rested his hand on the butt of the pistol tucked into his waistband at the small of his back. They spoke for a moment, and then she gestured for Joe and Charley to follow.

"He is the party chairman in the village," she whispered. "That's like a mayor in America."

The meeting hall was nothing more than a very large rectangular box. More than a dozen picnic tables with bench seats filled the middle of the room, more or less facing a long conference table and chairs that had been placed at the far end of room facing the audience. An imposing photo of Chairman Mao was hung on the back wall. The benches were crowded with people, while thirty or forty more stood quietly off to one side. They all watched the mayor lead the trio to the conference table. Smiling broadly, he urged them all to be seated. The mayor addressed the room for a brief moment and then said something to Vicki in Chinese before turning his attention to Joe.

"Sorry, I no speak English too good." He smiled again. "Dr. Xiao say you will come but not say when. We eat now, I think, and talk later."

At his signal, a parade of people suddenly appeared bearing platters of rice, steamed vegetables, roasted pork and duck, followed by pots of hot green tea. More chairs and tables were brought in to accommodate those standing along the wall. When every table had been served, the mayor filled Charley's plate with a generous sampling from each platter. No one touched their food. The villagers watched intently as Charley tasted a little of each dish before serving themselves. With a satisfied grin, he began eating with the ravenous appetite of a teenager. This seemed to evoke warm smiles and animated conversation from the previously stone-faced villagers. As if on cue, empty platters were quickly refilled and circulated around the room until both the hosts and their guests were satiated.

Finally, Vicki and Charley began making their rounds of the dinner tables with the mayor making introductions. Joe tagged along at a distance, fascinated, as he watched Charley speak with each villager in turn, shaking hands with some and bowing respectfully to others. The boy had the poise and easy camaraderie of a seasoned politician with these strangers.

The last of the villagers to be introduced was a painfully thin, somewhat feeble-looking old man. His wheelchair had decidedly seen better days, but his eyes sparkled when he spoke to Charley.

"This my grandfather." The mayor explained, speaking English for Joe's benefit. "He was born in Forbidden City in 1912 and lived there to 1924. He knew your grandfather."

Charley sat down beside him, and they spoke quietly for a while until it became too taxing for the old man to continue. They said goodbye and followed the mayor across the street.

"You will sleep my house tonight." He spoke plainly, leaving no room for discussion on this point. "My son, he put gas in your motorcycle so you start again early tomorrow morning."

They were escorted to the largest room in the mayor's house. It had been made up as a bedroom especially for the visitors. Of the two rather small beds, Vicki and Charley would share one while Joe would have to make do with the other. The boy barely got his shoes off before falling into a fitful sleep. Joe noted the small jade dragon in Charley's hand.

"Do you want some tea?" Vicki asked. She indicated the matched pair of handmade chairs standing beside a small table bearing a dim lamp and a pot of weak tea that completed the room's furnishings.

Joe sipped his tea and watched Charley for a few minutes before speaking.

"I don't understand how a single twelve-year-old boy could be such a threat to a political machine like the deputy minister of justice? What could Charley do to him or for him that would make Yung-Cheng risk everything to get him?"

"What did Wendy tell you?" Vicki asked.

"She thought that two or more groups would want to use Charley for political purposes. Maybe even use him in an effort to restore the empire."

"Maybe ..." She left the thought hanging in the air.

"You don't think so, do you?"

Vicki shrugged her shoulders, remaining silent and looking at the contents of her tea cup.

"Joe, how much do you know of China's recent history?"

"Not all that much, I guess."

"In 1912, the first Republic of China was established by Dr. Sun Yat-sen. Under the terms of a deal with the new republicans in the south, the Dowager Empress agreed that Puyi, he was Charley's grandfather, would abdicate the throne. The emperor was six years old and basically imprisoned in the Forbidden City while a civil war was about to be waged for control of China." She leaned across the table and continued to speak softly. "When Sun Yat-sen could not defeat General Yuan Shikai, they negotiated a deal to share power. The deal included the 1914 Articles of Abdication that specified the money and property to be given to Charley's grandfather as compensation."

Joe listened carefully without interrupting.

"It got more complicated after that," she continued. "By 1932, in an attempt to prevent war with Japan, the republican government agreed that Puyi would become the ruler of Manchuria under the Articles of Abdication. But when he was crowned emperor of Manchukuo in 1934 and declared to be under Japanese protection, the Chinese government labeled him a traitor and ordered his arrest."

"Okay, but what does that have to do with Charley and the deputy minister of justice?"

"I'm getting to that." Vicki was getting more animated. "A few years ago, the People's Republic of China decided to create free economic zones to help develop private enterprise. The central government passed a law allowing private ownership of land and recognizing all contracts, land titles, and treaties dating back well before the war."

"So, under this new law, someone could claim he owned the land his family has farmed for six hundred years and the government would give it to him?" he asked.

"Well, it's a little tougher than that, but yes." She sat back and waited.

"So, you're saying Charley can claim to be the emperor of Manchuria?"

"No. Technically, there is no empire, but Charley does own Manchuria. The claim is worth hundreds of billions of dollars."

"I guess that explains why Wei Yung-Cheng was willing to risk everything to get his hands on Charley," Joe observed. "Whoever controls Manchuria and its natural resources controls the economy of China."

"From Yung-Cheng's point of view, he has to have Charley alive or dead," Vicki pointed out. "Alive, he can petition the court claiming to be Charley's guardian. But if Charley is dead, he can substitute any twelve-year-old as the emperor's grandson."

"Why can't he do that anyway? He certainly has no problem having people killed. Is there any proof that Charley is the rightful heir?"

"When you visited the Forbidden City with Wendy, she took something out of a secret compartment in the back of the Dragon Throne. Do you remember?"

Joe nodded.

"Did you look inside?"

"I opened it after the police told me about Wendy's death."

"The Heirloom Seal of the Realm hasn't been seen in public for a thousand years. That's the proof. He either has to have it or destroy it." She leaned back in the chair.

"What are the chances that a people's court would recognize Charley's claim?"

198 FRANK R. HELLER

"It doesn't really matter. Even if the court denies the claim, it would still have a huge impact on China's economy and the world," Vicki said. "Besides, as deputy minister of justice, Wei Yung-Cheng has a lot of influence over the courts in China. Using Charley, he could literally blackmail the central government to get whatever he wanted."

Absently, Joe studied the remnants of his tea, evaluating their situation. The weight of the semiautomatic pistol in his jacket pocket was of little reassurance. He'd taken it from Yung-Cheng's thug to ease their escape. Now, he regretted leaving his original weapon on the bus. If they got trapped again by the Bai Lang, a single pistol would give them very little protection.

The facts were bleak. They were on the run, dependent on an underground organization for their survival. And they had no way of defending themselves if they were cornered again. The Bai Lang controlled the police and had his own private army. Their only hope was to make it to Shanghai. *Never give up!*

"We should get some sleep," he said, finally. "I want to get an early start in the morning."

TWENTY-TWO

CHOU LI QIANG SAT IN THE REAR SEAT OF THE BLACK SEDAN, watching the cars going in and out of the American embassy compound. He couldn't really see who was in any particular vehicle. He knew the gardener trimming flowers near the main entrance could not only see but also hear the instructions given to the driver. When the gardener pointed out Fitzpatrick's car, they followed it to the airport. After noting the trade delegate's flight to Shanghai, Chou Li Qing placed a quick call on his cell phone.

"Take my private plane. I will make the arrangements." The Bai Lang told Chou Li Qiang. "You will get to Shanghai twenty minutes ahead of our American friend."

LIKE FARMERS THE WORLD OVER, THE WORKDAY IN DR. XIAO'S village began with the first light of morning. By eight o'clock, only the mayor remained to see them off. He wished them good luck, shook their hands, and watched as the motorcycle moved along the narrow road toward the highway. When it was out of sight, he mumbled a little prayer on their behalf before turning away.

Back on the G-40 Expressway, traffic seemed lighter to Joe as he managed to work around a stream of heavy trucks. Perhaps at that hour of the morning, about midway between Xian and Shanghai, the heaviest traffic from either city hadn't caught up with them as yet. Joe pushed the distracting thoughts out of his mind and focused his attention on getting to Shanghai as quickly as possible. Once out of China, Charley and Vicki would be safe. Well, safer at least.

Despite the ebb and flow of traffic, traversing small villages and larger towns, they managed to make the seven-hour drive in just over five and a half hours. Joe took a convenient, if somewhat little used, exit off the expressway once they were well into the city. Pulling to the curb, he shut off the engine, tugged his helmet off, and leaned back to stretch for a moment.

"Do you know your way around this city?" he asked Vicki while scanning Dr. Xiao's map. "It's been a lot of years since my last visit."

"Actually, I do." She took the map, folded it, and shoved it in a pocket of the sidecar. "Go straight down this street for about six blocks. I'll tell you where to turn."

"Remember: we have to find a place to park the motorcycle."

"I think the hotel has a parking garage nearby."

Once underway again, Joe followed the Hankou Road, maneuvering through the heavy traffic.

"The next boulevard is Zhongshan East, you have to make a left turn onto that street. But be careful, it's loaded with tourists and a little tricky."

As they approached the intersection, the area was beginning to look familiar. Following her instructions, Joe turned left and continued for a few more blocks until they reached Nanjing Road. The Fairmont Peace Hotel was on the corner. Making another left turn, Joe drove past the entrance. At the end of the block, he turned down the ramp of the underground parking for the hotel.

Following the ramp all the way down to the bottom level, Joe found a small work area. It was the perfect place to park the motorcycle, somewhat hidden behind two pillars and a trash dumpster. They left the helmets, goggles, and gloves in the sidecar.

"It will probably be a few days before anyone notices the bike parked in this corner."

Vicki used what was left of their water and some paper towels to clean the road grime off their faces and hands. Joe pulled his blue jacket and ball cap out of the backpack. With a camera slung over his shoulder, the trio once again looked the part of a family of tourists.

Once on the street, they made their way along Nanjing Road toward the Bund. They walked casually, window shopping, seemingly without purpose, until they reached the entrance of the Peace Hotel. From the reception, Joe led them through the octagonal rotunda that served as the architectural hub of the hotel to the bank of elevators off to the right. They waited with several other guests for an empty car. Joe stood back until one of the other guests used his key card before pressing the button for the eighth floor.

"You know, the Dragon restaurant doesn't open until five thirty?" The guest commented.

"I just want the boy to see the view." Joe smiled while placing his hand on the pistol tucked into his waist band at the small of his back.

"Well, have a good time." The couple got off the elevator on the fifth floor.

The eighth-floor vestibule was deserted. Not wanting to waste time, Joe turned toward the entrance of the Dragon Phoenix restaurant. The doors were closed but not locked. Holding the door open, he waited for Vicki and Charley to step inside.

The Dragon Phoenix restaurant was an open and spacious affair with high, wide windows overlooking the Bund, crowded riverfront walk and the rest of city beyond. The room was filled with fifteen large tables covered with immaculate white linens. Three busboys were in the process of placing flatware and glasses on the tables getting them ready for the first dinner seating. Other than a quick glance, two of the workers ignored the intruders completely, while the third man watched them closely.

Joe finally spoke up, but the three workers still paid no attention. "We are meeting someone here." Finally, an older Chinese gentleman wearing a formal tuxedo came into the room through a pair of swinging doors off to the left. When he saw them standing by the reception desk, he rushed over smiling.

"I am so sorry to keep you waiting, but we are not yet open."

"We are meeting someone, a Mr. Fitzpatrick." That was all Joe needed to say.

"You are Mr. Wilder, no?" His demeanor changed instantly. "Through this room to the private room on the right." He gestured to the third busboy. "Tao will show you."

The private room occupied a full corner of the eighth floor. Among the twelve or fifteen tables in the room, Michael Fitzpatrick had chosen the one table with the greatest panoramic views of the Bund, the Shanghai skyline and the Huangpu River through two sets of windows.

"Good, you're on time." He got to his feet to greet them. "Please have a seat. We have a lot to go over and not much time." Fitzpatrick held a large manila envelope in his hand. "Would you like some tea?"

"No, thank you." Vicki declined for all of them.

"I guess not, Tao, thanks."

The busboy withdrew but remained standing outside the slightly open door to the private room.

"How are you doing, Charley?"

"I'm okay, Mr. Fitzpatrick." The boy made an attempt at a smile.

He was quiet for a moment, almost reluctant to get down to the business at hand.

"Your cruise cards in the names of Joe, Vicki, and Charley Thomas are in here." He handed Joe the envelope.

"What cruise cards?" Joe emptied the envelope on the table.

"I'm getting you out of the country on a cruise ship. It's the only way. They check your passport when you walk into an airport, at the check-in counter and again when you board the plane. On a ship, security will scan these cards before you can board. That's all. And when they do, your pictures will come up on their computer just like every other passenger."

"How is that possible?" Vicki asked, but he just smiled.

"As far as the ship and her crew is concerned, you have been on board for the entire cruise. I had your suitcases put in your stateroom last night." Next, Fitzpatrick picked up three airline tickets. "The ship will spend one day at sea and then dock in Inchon, South Korea, at eight o'clock in the morning day after tomorrow."

"What then?" Joe asked.

"You get a taxi and head for the airport. You're booked on American Airlines to Los Angeles. First class, I might add." Putting everything back in the envelope, he handed it to Joe. "I'll be there waiting when you land. You do have your passports?" It was almost an afterthought.

"I have mine," Joe replied.

"And I have Charley's and mine," Vicki added.

They spent the next fifteen minutes discussing the details of getting on board the ship in Shanghai and making the transfer to the airport in Seoul. Finally, he handed Joe an electronic room key.

"You're in suite 766. There are fresh clothes, toiletries, and everything you need to look like cruise ship tourists coming back from a day of sightseeing." He paused for a long moment before going on, unsure if he should speak in front of the boy or not.

"What is it?" Joe asked, sensing his hesitation. "Charley can hear anything you need to say."

"You made quite an impression on our friend the deputy minister of justice at the Terracotta Museum."

"Really? And how is the great White Wolf these days?"

"He's pissed and turning the country upside down looking for you." Fitzpatrick toyed with his empty tea cup. "He figures that Vicki and Charley can disappear into the population without too much trouble. So you're his only lead to find them. When he gets his hands on you he won't be too worried about your Miranda rights before questioning. And when he's done, he'll kill you just for the fun of it."

"How do you know all this?" Joe asked.

"We had someone inside his team."

"Had?"

"Yeah, after your boating accident on the Yellow River and the mess in Xian, our contact turned up dead this morning. That's the second one. We think he was blamed for your escape." He left that information hanging in the air. "Okay, you have a little time to get cleaned up. But you have to be on board no later than nine tonight. The ship sails at ten."

They got to their feet to say goodbye and shook hands. On an impulse, Vicki reached up and put her arms around Fitzpatrick's neck, giving him a hug.

"Thank you for all your help." With that, she turned and led the way out of the restaurant. As they disappeared through the door, Michael Fitzpatrick, who hadn't been in church since his days as an altar boy, said a little prayer under his breath.

"God knows they're not out of trouble yet."

TAO WATCHED THEM GO OUT THE RESTAURANT DOORS TO THE elevator. As nonchalantly as possible, he pulled out a cell phone, pressed a button on the speed dial, and waited. When it was answered, he spoke softly into the phone, repeating the conversation he had just overheard.

TWENTY-THREE

Shanghai's new international cruise ship terminal was a marvel of glass, steel, and modern architecture. Resembling a giant bubble, the multiple-building complex consists of hotels, shops, offices and condominiums. Passenger facilities are on the main and lower levels with elevated walkways to board the ships. The taxi drop-off area was chaos, with hundreds of tourists returning to the three cruise ships docked at the international terminal. As surreptitiously as possible, Joe wrapped the pistol in a wade of tissues and dropped it in a trash can before they entered the building.

"We just have to follow the signs for the *Dream Princess*," Joe explained as they maneuvered through the crowd.

Once in the main lobby, signs directed passengers along various access routes to board each ship. The last security checkpoint for their ship before boarding was on the lower level. Glancing around the hallways as they walked, Joe tried not to be too obvious as he watched for signs of trouble.

The terminal was awash with security personnel and some city police, but that wasn't a problem. He was worried about the Bai Lang's Ministry of Justice officers they faced in Xian.

Finally, they were next in line to go through the checkpoint. Their backpacks and Vicki's purse went through the scanner without setting off any alarms. Joe heaved a sigh of relief when they grabbed everything and started to walk down the hallway.

"Do you think I could have a word with you before you leave Shanghai?" A grim-faced Police Inspector Chou Kong-Sang stepped out of the shadows followed by Detective Yuen Woo and several uniformed officers. "There is a private room just down the hall and to the right where we can talk."

Joe felt the sudden rush of adrenaline. Clenching his fists, he considered making a fight of it. He could take out the inspector and Detective Woo, but there were too many police and security officers nearby. Silently, they followed the inspector into a sterile-looking room furnished with a single long table and six chairs. While the six uniformed officers took up positions at the two doors and around the room, Inspector Chou removed his suit jacket and took a seat at the table.

"Please be seated." He opened a thick file and spread the pages out on the table. "It seems that you have had a very troubled visit to China. Let's see, the two men on the Skewed Tobacco Pouch Street, the incident on the Great Wall and then the Terracotta Warriors Museum. The body count is rising." He stared at Charley for a long moment. "What should we do with you?"

Before Joe could reply, the door was suddenly thrown open, banging against the wall. The deputy minister of justice strode triumphantly into the room. Two uniformed Ministry of Justice security officers and the German followed closely behind. Standing at the end of the table, grinning at them malevolently, he said something to Inspector Chou in Chinese that made Vicki grab Charley protectively.

"Tell this strutting peacock that if he makes one move toward Charley, I will snap his neck before your people can even think about stopping me." Joe spoke softly, almost in a whisper.

"You are not in a position to make threats, Mr. Wilder!" The deputy minister of justice shouted in English. "You will do what you are told and nothing more. If you cooperate, I might let you leave China alive!" When he started to walk around the table toward Charley, Detective Woo stepped forward to block his movement. And suddenly, Max, the dangerous German, seemed very nervous.

"You know, Deputy Minister, this is still my case." The inspector pulled some more sheets of paper from his file. "I am responsible for solving a series of murders as well as several other very serious crimes. And, as a matter of fact, I think I have solved almost all of those cases."

"And you know who I am, Inspector?" His level of rage was beginning to rise to the boiling point.

"Oh, yes, Deputy Minister, I have been looking into your records very carefully." Inspector Chou began rolling up his shirt sleeves as he rose to face the man. "And I realized that you, Wei Yung-Cheng, are a traitor to the People's Republic of China. You are personally responsible for the deaths of more than a hundred people. You have been poisoning our children with your illegal drugs for years, and you are guilty of attempting to murder a highly respected American business man visiting our country!" He shot a quick warm smile at Joe before continuing. "And so, Mr. Bai Lang, Mr. White Wolf, you are under arrest!"

"Are you crazy? What are you talking about?" Wei Yung-Cheng went pale as two police officers roughly slammed him down on the table and snapped the handcuffs in place. Other officers quickly disarmed and handcuffed the security officers as well. At that moment, knowing that he was next, Max reached for the gun at his waist. Detective Woo was quicker, firing a Taser that instantly disabled the man.

"Detective Woo, please give the order to arrest the remaining members of the Bai Lang's inner circle."

When they were finally dragged from the room, leaving Inspector Chou and the three people seated before him alone.

"My apologies for the interruption. I see from your cruise documents that you are Mr. and Mrs. Joe Thomas, traveling with your son, Charley." His smile carried a reassuring warmth as he handed back their cruise cards and closed the file.

"I don't understand?" Joe said finally. "What happened?"

"It's really very simple. We believe in justice, real justice, just like in America. We can't let the bad guys get away with anything."

The inspector pulled up his shirtsleeve to expose the imperial dragon tattoo on his forearm and leaned forward to speak softly. "Besides, we are sworn to protect the Son of Heaven."

"Thank you." Charley smiled in return.

"It is my honor to be able to help you."

THEIR CABIN WAS A PORT-SIDE MINISUITE WITH A PRIVATE BALCONY on the Caribe Deck. From their vantage point, standing at the railing sipping champagne, Vicki and Joe watched the city of Shanghai slide by as the *Dream Princess* made its way down the Huangpu River toward the East China Sea.

"It really is a beautiful city." Joe refilled her glass.

"Yes, it is." She was silent for a few minutes when Charley joined them on the balcony. Leaning on the railing, they watched the city lights. After a few minutes, Charley turned toward them with a sad expression on his face.

"Are we ever going to come back to China?"

"I hope so, someday." It was all Vicki could say. She put her arm around Charley's shoulder.

"Once we get to the states and after everything has calmed down here, let's see if Mr. Fitzpatrick can work something out."

The boy went back inside the cabin and sprawled on the bed to watch television.

"What do we do now?" She asked.

"Well, for starters, we can spend the next thirty-six hours relaxing and having a little fun," Joe said, laughing. "We don't need to keep looking over our shoulders any more. And, thanks to Inspector Chou Kong-Sang, there won't be anyone else trying to hurt Charley."

"That is true." She returned his smile. "And that is thanks to you."

"After a peaceful night's sleep, we can enjoy a great breakfast and a day at sea with very little to do but relax and get to know each other better."

"I will drink to that!" She raised her glass in a toast.

It was nearly three o'clock in the morning as Michael Fitzpatrick sat in the ops center conference room waiting for his call. As usual, he was nursing a cup of black coffee that was much too hot to drink. In fact, he thought it needed a shot of good Irish whiskey to be drinkable at all. When the intercom buzzed, he lifted the receiver and waited.

"Your call is on line one, Mr. Fitzpatrick."

"Thanks, Susan." He pressed line one and waited again.

"Well, Michael, how did our boy do?"

"He did it all, Mr. President. If he was in the Marines, you could say he improvised, adapted, and overcame." *Once a Marine, always a Marine,* Fitzpatrick thought. "They are on their way to Inchon as we speak, sir."

"I'm happy to hear that, Michael." The president chuckled into the phone. "No lie, I was a little concerned when Wendy chose an over-the-hill, out-of-shape businessman for the job."

"Yes, sir, but from what I've seen, we could use a few more just like him."

"All right, let's give them a week or so in LA until we see which way the Chinese government handles the situation. Then we'll bring them to Washington."

"It shouldn't be a problem, sir. Beijing was very happy to be able to ferret out the crooked deputy minister of justice. And, don't forget, they knocked out a major source of illegal drugs coming into China at the same time. I think they will be happy to make it a joint operation as far as the public is concerned."

"Well done, Michael. Call me when you get them settled in LA."

TWENTY-FOUR

THIRTY-SIX HOURS AT SEA UNDER BEAUTIFULLY CLEAR, SUNNY SKIES on board the newest ship in the fleet was not exactly torture. The *Dream Princess* was designed to compete with the most luxurious ships of other cruise lines. It wasn't exactly the trip he had planned, but Joe had to admit it had been a remarkable adventure.

He got up before dawn, careful not to disturb either of his traveling companions, in order to climb the steps leading to the highest observation point on the ship. He found a cushion from a deck chair and propped it up against the bulkhead. Leaning back, he sipped the hot, black coffee he'd brought along and watched the sun slowly rise above the eastern horizon. Joe calculated that he'd taken at least eighteen or twenty cruises over the years. Watching the sunrise his first day at sea had become something of a personal tradition that never seemed to lose its appeal.

After breakfast, they spent most of the morning touring the ship. Charley seemed to take a special interest in the shops that were loaded with merchandise of every kind. When they reached the fitness center, Joe commented on how long it has been since he worked out. But no one seemed interested, not even him. Finally, Vicki suggested they have lunch by the pool on the Lido Deck.

"Charley, you know there's a youth center just one deck up?" Joe said.

"I know." He dipped a french fry in ketchup.

"Do you want to see if there are some kids your age to meet?"

"No, thanks, it's not for me. They have some video games and a pool table, but I'd rather read. The ship has a great library." Charley moved to a lounge chair and buried his nose in a book.

They finished lunch in silence, each seemingly lost in thought. Eventually, Joe appeared to have reached a decision.

"Okay, you're going to stay with me until things get settled."

"Cool!" Charley smiled happily.

"I guess if you insist." There was a definite sparkle in her eyes. Joe noticed.

"But the more important question is what are you going to do afterward? I know I asked this before, but do you have a plan?"

"I suppose Wendy had some arrangements, but I have no idea what she had in mind," Vicki said. "Frankly, I haven't thought that far ahead."

"Well, I have given it a lot of thought." He turned in his chair to face her. "You're going to stay with me for as long as you like."

"I think you just said that." A broad smile was tugging at the corners of her mouth.

"Okay, just making sure." He grinned. "We need to get Charley registered for school—he's so bright, they will probably have trouble figuring out where to place him. And, I guess you will need to get a job of some kind." Joe toyed with the silverware distractedly. "I'm sure Fitzpatrick can arrange for the work permits."

"I don't think that will be a problem." It was the first time since they met that she came close to laughing.

"I guess I could hire you as a translator at Wilder Enterprises given how much business we do with China." Then almost as an afterthought, he asked if Wendy had left any money for Charley.

"It's not a problem, Joe." Now she was laughing. "When Charley's grandfather was crowned emperor by the Dowager Empress Cixi in 1908, he was a little more than two and half years old. The empress knew that she was already sick and afraid there would be a revolution after she died. To safeguard the young emperor, she established the EEF with the help of the American government." She paused so Joe could absorb it all.

"What is the EEF?"

"She called it the Emperor's Escape Fund." Vicki laughed out loud. "I guess she had a sense of humor after all. That money now belongs to Charley."

"Are you sure the money is still there?" he asked.

"From 1908 until now, the funds have been invested over the years with certain guarantees from the US government."

"How much money are you talking about?"

"The last time we talked about it, Wendy said the fund was nearly three hundred million US dollars. Your friend Mr. Fitzpatrick knows all about it."

ACCORDING TO THE SHIP'S CALENDAR OF EVENTS, DINNER TONIGHT, while not a formal evening, was going to be a little swankier than normal. The cabin steward gave them directions to their table for the second seating in the Da Vinci Dining Room.

"What should I order?" Charley asked, looking over the menu.

"Anything you want and as much as you want." Joe noticed that New England lobster was offered, either boiled, broiled, or stuffed. "Have you ever had lobster?"

"No, I never tried it."

"I love it!" Vicki said. "But it can get messy."

"I'll tell you what, Charley," Joe offered. "I'll order the lobster and give you some to taste."

"I think I'll just have the steak." The boy closed his menu and sat back comfortably.

"Me too," Vicki chimed in.

When the waiter came to take their orders, Joe couldn't help commenting.

"I'm traveling with a couple of carnivores!"

They enjoyed the meal immensely. It was unhurried and relaxed. A first since they had met a week earlier. The conversation was animated and wide reaching. They talked sports, international politics, and Charley's ambitions for the future. At twelve, he wasn't certain what career path he would ultimately choose, but UCLA was definitely one of his goals. As to football, it was strictly a spectator sport. And preferably on television. On the other hand, when it came to baseball, Charley was a Dodger fan all the way.

"Well, this may come as a shock to you, Charley." Joe tried to hide his sheepish grin. "I have season tickets at Dodger Stadium." This announcement started a totally new discussion on sports, amid speculation that the Dodgers might make it to the World Series this year.

When the waiter finally brought dessert menus, the only item that seemed interesting was the hot fudge sundae.

"Have you ever had one?"

"Joe!" Charley rolled his eyes, giving him a withering look. "It was invented in China by King Tang in the seventh century! Ice cream, not hot fudge."

"Oh, I'm sorry. I didn't realize you were that old," Joe said with a straight face. "But do you want one?"

"No, I'm too full."

"All right. Let's skip dessert," Vicki said. "There is a show in the Princess Theater. Do you want to go?"

They managed to find good seats on the aisle in the tenth row. Charley was a little skeptical at first, but it turned out to be a rock-and-roll musical review. Individual ship's crew members impersonated Elvis, Jerry Lee Lewis, Buddy Holly, Chuck Berry, Connie Francis, Lesley Gore, and Mary Wells. They joined together to recreate the great groups of the 1950s and 1960s, ending with a Beatles finale.

They walked back to the cabin at a leisurely pace. It was nearly midnight when they got Charley settled in bed. The boy was too tired to read the book sitting on his night table.

"Are you totally exhausted?" Joe asked.

"Not really." Vicki looked at him curiously. "Why?"

"Well, there's a lounge on the Promenade deck."

"Yes?" She asked.

The realization that she was flirting with him came as a pleasant surprise.

"They have a bar, a good band, and a dance floor. Would you like to celebrate a little?"

The band in the Explorer's Lounge played a wide range of music designed to appeal to the median age group of the passengers on board. Joe ordered two glasses of Grand Marnier and waited for a slow song before asking Vicki on the dance floor.

"You dance very well," she said after a few minutes.

"Oh, no. I've got three left feet, and they're all on my right side!" Joe looked down and smiled at her. "You just make me look good."

They danced for quite a while, mostly to slow songs. It felt so good to hold Vicki in his arms that he was reluctant to let go. He didn't want to let either of them go.

"You make me feel good, Joe."

When they finally decided to call it a night, it was just past two o'clock in the morning.

"Would you like to go out on deck for a few minutes before we go in?" He asked. She simply nodded in response.

Walking out on the port side, they turned aft toward the fantail. It was a beautiful, clear night. The moon was full, and the sky was filled with a million stars undiluted by ambient city lights. Standing at the fantail railing, Joe pointed out the shimmering phosphorescent glimmer of the ship's wake. The iridescent glow trailed the ship for more than a mile.

"What is it?" she asked.

"It's an ocean algae, small plankton, churned up by the ship's propellers," he explained.

"I've never seen anything like that. It's beautiful!" She turned toward him.

The moonlight made her face glow and her eyes sparkle with a captivating iridescent quality of their own. Joe reached up and caressed her cheek lightly.

"You are so beautiful." Leaning over, he kissed her softly on the lips. Without breaking the kiss, but adding her own passion, Vicki wrapped her arms around his neck and held on tight. "I don't want to lose you."

Their mood was suddenly broken by the sound of someone tripping over a deck chair in the dark area behind them. Joe turned around in time to see a heavyset man moving warily toward them. He was big, barrel chested, and looked to be solidly built. The man moved in a menacing way that reminded Joe of a wrestler looking for an opening against an opponent.

"Is there something you want?" Joe asked, gently pushing Vicki to the left, away from the threat.

"What did you do with the Bai Lang?" Chou Li Qiang asked.

"The Bai Lang is in jail," Joe stated flatly. "Who the hell are you?"

"My name is Chou Li Qiang." The man began to circle to his right along the railing. "Remember it because I am going to kill you!"

A sudden movement in the big man's right hand caught Joe's attention. A long-bladed knife flashed briefly in the moonlight. Joe pushed Vicki farther off to the side.

"Why would you want to kill me? What did I do to you?" He was buying time, looking for an opening to disarm the man. Obviously, he had been drinking, but the man wasn't drunk enough. He was still dangerous.

"You, that woman, and the boy—you are the reason the Bai Lang took so many chances. Now he's in jail and everything we worked for is gone." Chou Li Qiang began edging closer along the railing. Squaring his body, the would-be attacker crouched slightly, shifting his weight from side to side and bringing the knife up, ready to lunge forward.

Joe waited for the thrust of the knife that he knew was coming. When it came, the attacker would be off balance for a second or two with his arm extended. That would be the opportunity he needed.

The lunge came suddenly, with the man's full weight behind the blade. Joe sidestepped, grabbing the outstretched arm in both hands. Rotating his body, Joe slammed himself and the assailant against the rail. He caught the angle just right, snapping the man's elbow with a sickening sound. Chou Li Qiang screamed in pain as the knife dropped to the deck. Turning again, Joe drove his knee into his attacker's groin, doubling him over. A final fist to the jaw left him unconscious and momentarily out of pain.

Vicki had run back inside, calling for help. By the time the Master at Arms—the ship's police—arrived, the fight was over. Chou Li Qiang was treated for his injuries and locked in the brig. At Joe's insistence, the captain placed a phone call to Inspector Chou Kong-Sang. Arrangements would be made to extradite the career criminal back to China when they docked at Inchon.

Back in the cabin when it was all over, Joe sat beside Charley and recounted the evening's events.

"What exactly does all this mean?" Charley asked. Joe sensed the boy wasn't sure if he should be frightened or relieved.

"It means that the Bai Lang and the Bai Lang army are done. They will never bother you again."

TWENTY-FIVE

THE *DREAM PRINCESS* DOCKED AT THE PORT OF INCHON, SOUTH Korea, at precisely 8:00 a.m. Two hours later, Joe was tipping the skycap who'd checked their luggage onto the flight to Los Angeles and directed them to security and passport control. By noon, they were wheels up and turning east on the final leg of their journey.

"Good morning, ladies and gentlemen." The pilot's disembodied voice sounded soothing over the PA system. "Our flight time to Los Angeles today will be a little more than ten hours and fifteen minutes. We have clear skies all the way, so please sit back and enjoy your flight."

It took Charley only ten minutes to discover all the hidden joys of his first-class seat pod. By the time Joe checked on him, he had the headphones on and was deeply engrossed in deciding which movie he was going to watch first. On the other hand, Vicki and Joe took advantage of the long flight to talk. Endlessly, it seemed. It was the equivalent of a first and second date in international airspace.

"If you're going to be living with me, I think we should get better acquainted." After all, he did sound reasonable.

"Are you sure you want us to live with you?" Now she was being coy? But he smiled and said he was certain.

After four meals, snacks, fresh chocolate chip cookies, and endless movies and videos on their personal at-your-seat screens, the flight finally touched down at Los Angeles International Airport just shy of ten fifteen in the evening. Loaded down with their carry-on bags, Joe led them along the skyway and into the terminal. Michael Fitzpatrick was waiting just inside the doorway.

"So how was the flight?" he asked, shaking Joe's hand and not waiting for a reply. "We're going to take you through the VIP gate at passport control and customs." He grinned at Charley. "After all, you are a visiting dignitary."

At the desk, the ICE agent examined their passports and then, with a smile and a flourish, stamped each passport and slid them across the counter.

"Welcome to the United States, and welcome home, Mr. Wilder."

It took no more than fifteen minutes for them to get through the VIP line at customs. The long corridor leading to the front of the international terminal was lined with display cases exhibiting fashions from world-famous designers and department stores and the best from student design competitions.

"What are all these things?" Charley asked, indicating the displays.

"Well, these are fashions made by designers from all over the world. Some are from manufacturers here in Los Angeles, and some are student designs from local colleges. And there are some department store displays too," Fitzpatrick explained.

"Oh." Walking slowly along the corridor, Charley seemed to study the dresses in each of the cases.

Further down the hallway, Charley stopped to look at a large showcase exhibiting several samples of contemporary young women's fashions for teenagers. After a long pause, Charley said something to Vicki in Chinese.

"Sure, anytime you want," she replied in English, laughing.

"What was that all about?" Joe asked.

"Charley asked if it was all right to wear dresses now that we are really in America." She leveled her gaze directly at Joe. His mouth opened and closed several times, but he was unable to speak.

"Joe, Charley is a girl!" Taking his arm, they continued to walk toward the entrance of the building and Joe's waiting limousine.

"As the heir of the last emperor, Wendy knew her only child would be in danger eventually. Or, at the very least, a target for some political group. The official records show that Wendy had one child and that child was a girl. So she decided—we all decided—that it would be safer to raise Charley as a boy, at least as far as everyone outside our family knew. The problem was that as she grew into puberty it would have been harder to hide Charley's gender. Coming to America now means the difference between life and death." Vicki stopped walking and looked directly into Joe's eyes.

"And, thanks to you, it means that Charley will have a very good and, hopefully, a very long and happy life."

It took a minute or two to sink in, and then Joe smiled warmly and turned to Charley.

"All this time I've been thinking how good it would feel to have you as a son. But the truth is that I've always dreamt of having a daughter."

Charley wrapped her arms around Joe's neck and hugged him tightly.

"I guess this means that you are the secret empress of China!"

Printed in the United States
By Bookmasters